THE END

For Telf:
RIP

Acknowledgments

Thanks to Ian Whates for asking me to write this, and to Ians Whates and Watson for helping me whip the rushed first draft into shape; to Charlie and Emily (as always) for keeping me sane; to whoever told me about the BBC news footage that inspired the prologue; to all my writer friends (you know who you are) for giving me a creative lifeline away from the day job; to Gary Fry for giving me an idea I'd not thought of; to my good friend Mark West for providing some vital comments on the story at short notice; and to my family for continuing to believe in me – even during those times when I no longer believe in myself.

THE END

Gary McMahon

NewCon Press
England

First published in the UK by NewCon Press
41 Wheatsheaf Road, Alconbury Weston, Cambs, PE28 4LF

NCP 079 (limited edition hardback)
NCP 080 (softback)

10 9 8 7 6 5 4 3 2 1

ISBN:

978-1-907069-20-8 (hardback)
978-1-900669-21-5 (softback)

Cover layout and design by Andy Bigwood

Edited by Ian Whates and Ian Watson
Book layout by Storm Constantine

Like as the waves make towards the pebbl'd shore,
so do our minutes, hasten to their end...

Sonnet LX
William Shakespeare

ONE:
THE FIRST WAVE

Christy was driving – she always drove, because Kath was incapable of getting behind the wheel of any vehicle without causing some kind of accident. It was almost noon, and she was hungry. They hadn't eaten a thing since late last night, after too far many beers in The Haycart with all the gang who couldn't make it to the wedding.

Christy's baby brother, Ben, was finally doing it – tying the knot. Christy could barely believe it, even now, on their way to Dover to catch a ferry across the Channel. It seemed like some ridiculous joke: her clumsy, thoughtless younger brother getting married to a gorgeous, sophisticated French girl with rich parents.

She looked across at Kath, who was staring ahead at the motorway traffic, lost in the depths of her hangover. Kath had always had a thing for Ben; for years she'd crushed on him, even when he went away to work in Paris and then Normandy, for the firm owned by his beloved Francesca's parents. Kath wasn't taking the news well, but she was at least grateful to have been invited to the wedding.

Christy looked back at the road. Traffic was heavy but not unusually so. The sky was dull and overcast, a typical autumn day. She stared at the slow-moving traffic in the opposite lane. People sat with their windows rolled down, cigarette smoke drifting out of the gaps. Children argued in rear seats.

She indicated and crossed over into the fast lane, overtaking some old codger driving a shitty little Nissan. She stared at the driver as she passed the car. His old, creased face was locked into position, his bespectacled eyes not moving from the windscreen. Why did all old people drive like that, as if their necks had been broken and they couldn't turn their heads to the side?

She drifted back into the slow lane. Beside her, Kath retuned the radio to a channel playing soft rock – Poison, Bon Jovi, Mötley Crüe, all those tacky bands from the eighties they'd both adored. Kath began to sing along: 'Every Rose Has its Thorn".

Too true, thought Christy. Too bloody true.

She was leaving behind her a good-looking boyfriend who didn't really give a shit about her needs and a job she hated. Ben had intimated that he might be able to hook her up with a job in the firm, and she was starting to believe that this could be the start of better things, nicer times. God knew, she deserved something. When their mother died, she became the parent, looking after Ben until he was old enough to strike out on his own. Only, he'd struck out too far, hadn't he, and left her behind? Now it was time for him to repay the debt, to send some love her way.

She smiled. He was a good brother – she'd always known he'd do something with his life, which was why she'd abandoned her own ambitions to allow him every advantage.

The sky began to darken; fat clouds scudded across the vast grey expanse, filled with storm. Christy shivered, and tried to relax her shoulders. She was tired; the hangover was giving her a headache and she needed something to eat. "Should we stop soon? Get a sarnie or something?"

Kath nodded. "Might be a good idea. I'm starving."

The Nissan she'd overtaken was way behind, but now an estate car towing a large caravan was gaining on them. Who the hell took a caravan somewhere in autumn? Christy shook her head, bit her lower lip, and pressed her foot down on the accelerator.

The steering wheel spun away in her hands, tugging to the right; at the same time, there came a sharp popping noise somewhere just outside the car.

"Shit!" yelled Kath. "What's that?"

Christy fought to regain control of the car and, as it swerved into the outside lane, she realised the problem. "Flat tyre! It's a blow-out."

She braked steadily, not wanting to cause a skid, pulled the car back over into the inside lane and switched on her hazard lights. Horns sounded; other traffic flashed their lights. Christy focused on guiding the car to a halt on the hard shoulder.

Once the car had stopped, she managed to prise her fingers off the wheel. She was sweating; pure alcohol bled from the pores of her forehead and armpits. "Shit. That was scary."

"You're telling me…" Kath leaned over, clutching Christy's knee. "You okay, babe? You did well, you know."

Christy opened her eyes, glanced at her friend, and smiled. "Yeah, but now we need to change the sodding tyre."

They got out of the car.

Outside, Christy opened the boot and took out the spare tyre. Her heart was beating normally now. The panic was over. She rolled the spare across the narrow blacktopped shoulder and let it topple onto its side near the front of the car, then returned to the boot for the tools. She located the jack and the wheel brace, and then walked back to the front.

"Will this take long?" Kath was loitering outside the passenger door. She'd lit up a cigarette and was blowing smoke into the gloomy air. Her eyes were wide; the pupils were dilated.

"You just stand there and watch, eh? Leave this all to me."

"That's nice of you," said Kath, matching her sarcasm.

Christy began to loosen the wheel nuts. It took her almost fifteen minutes to jack up the car and manoeuvre the wheel off the axle.

She glanced up, at the sky, and hoped that it wouldn't rain – not while she was *squatting at the side of the road with her arse in the dirt.*

Once the wheel was off she swapped it for the spare. Then she stood and inspected her handiwork, rather proud of what she'd done. It was the first time she had ever changed a tyre on her own, and the sense of pride took her by surprise. Maybe she could make a go of things, after all. Start a new life, near her brother.

She knelt down by the tyre, reaching out a hand to touch the rubber…and that was when it happened: a slight tweaking sensation at the back of her head, like someone flicking her skull just above the nape of her neck. Only deeper, as if the flicking finger was inside her head instead of outside, and making direct contact with her brain. It lasted only a second – possibly even less than that – but when it was over she felt different somehow. What was she doing here, at the side of the road?

She looked up, at her friend, and Kath nodded. The cigarette burned between her fingers, smouldering down to the filter. Kath's eyes had turned dark: they were all pupil. The two girls stayed like that for a while, just staring at each other, and then, finally, as if in response to some unheard command, they both nodded again.

Kath flicked away her cigarette butt. Her eyes were black now, like pieces of coal.

Christy stood and stared at the passing shapes – traffic: that was the name. It was moving quickly, speeding by in a blur. Lunch hour traffic: heavier and faster than before. Even the vehicles in the opposite lanes were moving faster now.

The girls held hands instinctively, as if reaching out for support, and without further pause they stepped out – or lunged, for their movements were purposeful and aggressive – into the traffic.

Cars swerved; horns brayed; drivers shouted and raised their fists. A white van clipped Kath's left leg, breaking it at the knee and sending the lower part spinning around the fractured axis. Kath staggered but did not fall; she kept on moving across the lanes.

Christy squeezed her friend's hand, and took long, even strides, almost pulling her over. Whenever a car moved to avoid them, she readjusted her direction and tried to get hit. For some reason this was all she wanted: she needed to be hit by one of the vehicles. Nothing else mattered, just the impact. The nullification death would bring.

Neither of the girls spoke, not even when the occupants of stopped vehicles ran towards them and tried to drag them to safety. They fought back, lashing out at their would-be saviours, trying to lunge into the traffic.

Kath hobbled towards the central reservation, clambered over the low metal crash barrier, and flung herself into the path of a coach. Her body was pulled swiftly under the wheels and torn apart like a rag doll: arms and legs separated from her splitting torso, and a red spray painted the road surface. The coach screeched to a gradual halt, brakes singing. The passengers pressed their faces against the windows, trying to catch sight of the carnage behind.

Christy punched the man who held her, his attention diverted by Kath's fate. Her fist crunched against his cheek and he instinctively loosened his grip. She pulled away and ran back along the motorway, zigzagging into the oncoming traffic and urging them to mow her down.

It did not take long for her wish to be answered.

CHAPTER 1

This is how the world ends.

CHAPTER 2

Regent's Park was busy, as I supposed it must always be during office lunch hours. Secretaries in knee-length skirts and white blouses ate toasted Italian sandwiches from greaseproof paper bags; men in suits talked on mobile phones and stuffed overfilled burgers into their mouths between words. Old people sat on benches eating dried fruit and looking at the flowers. Dog-walkers made circles on the grass and tried to balance small plastic bags and crisp packets filled with shit on the palms of their hands while being dragged along by their eager hounds.

It seemed like the whole of London was crammed into that one park, and Mitch and I were lost souls amid the seething mass of humanity.

"I actually hate this place," said Mitch, carefully unwrapping his ham and cheese toasty. "Too many people for my liking."

"I could say the same about the whole of London." I smiled and took a bite out of my cold falafel, not particularly enjoying the harsh, dry taste as it filled my mouth.

"Yeah," said Mitch. "Sometimes I can see the appeal of living up there with you in the back o' beyond. Must be... quieter. Nobody to spoil the views."

I balled up the remains of my food and pitched it at a nearby bin. I didn't want to get up and place it inside, as an old woman with light blue hair and an angry face was hovering near our bench, looking for an opening. "It's better than this, anyway."

Mitch nodded.

I was missing Kay. I always missed Kay when I was away on business, especially when the business was down here, in the capital. We had a small cottage in West Yorkshire, out on the moors, and far enough from the nearest small town to be considered isolated. I'd been afraid at first, due to Kay's blindness, but she spent a long time reassuring me and telling me that it was what she'd always wanted: to live in the countryside, far away from people.

I'd come round in the end – of course I had; she was my wife, and if it made her happy then I was in – but still, whenever I had to be away from home, I felt guilty. But we settled quickly into a routine, and being one of the company directors I only had to go into the office in Leeds twice a week.

"How many months along is she now?" Mitch had finished his sandwich, and his question made me think that he'd been reading my thoughts.

"What?" I stared at him, blinking.

"Kay. The pregnancy. How many months along is she?" He smiled, his blue eyes sparkling.

"Six months. Long enough that I hate being away from her... even if it's for something as important as this." I smiled, but knew I probably wasn't too convincing.

Mitch nodded; he understood. Despite his own marriage potentially breaking down – or perhaps because of it – he knew how important mine was to me. I never had to explain to Mitch how Kay always came first. That was a given, and there was never any debate on the matter. We'd known each other long enough to be completely honest about our lives, and being business partners had actually increased the depth of that mutual understanding.

I eyed the old woman until she shrugged her shoulders and walked away, and then stared out at the people who were hurrying along their own paths, coming and going like little trains between unknown stations. City people all looked the same to me: squinted eyes, furrowed brows, tight features. The worries of urban life seemed to manifest on their flesh; a weird physical deformity noticed only by outsiders.

"We'll need to shove off soon. The meeting's scheduled to reconvene at two." Mitch looked tired. I wondered if he'd been sleeping much. Things were going badly, for us and for every other small business in the country, and the lack of firm orders was dragging us down. His marriage problems simply added to the stress. We'd studied together at University, got our degrees together, and started out working for the same tiny architectural firm in Bradford. I'd learned early how to read his moods, and this one was certainly murky.

"It'll be fine," I said. "We'll win this order. Why would they have called us down here if they didn't want to commission us for the design?" I stared at the side of his head until he turned to face me. "Am I right or am I right?"

He smiled, and the stress seemed to fall away... but only for a moment.

Mitch was a fine Architect and an even better friend; he worked on prestigious multi-million pound projects, was very good at his job and provided well financially for his family – despite his many infidelities, he always went back to his wife. In his own way, he loved her more than anything, but right now that love had become warped, and neither of them seemed to know what they wanted.

He was a good and constant companion, and I miss him dearly. I miss them all, everyone we lost during those first few days… and, of course, the ones who fell after. In many ways the ones we lost after the initial event were even harder to take.

I glanced up, squinting against the sun. It was a sharp day in October. Bright sunlight shone against the brown-leaved trees, belying the chill in the air. The sky was low and blue, and veined with scrappy white clouds. The office where we had been holed up all morning was near Baker Street. You could see Lords cricket ground from the boardroom window. The street outside was quiet for central London, despite its proximity to Regent's Park. I'd been in worse places in this city, but still I felt on edge. London did that to me – always made me feel as if something bad was about to happen.

Mitch began to stand, his knees bending and one arm going up and out to support himself on the same litter bin where I'd deposited my rubbish. Right then it seemed as if the whole park went silent for less than a second – the time it took for Mitch to go from sitting to crouching – and then that sudden and intense silence was filled, no *shattered*, by the sound of screaming.

"What?" Mitch looked about, trying to locate the source of the sound.

I tilted my head and narrowed my eyes. The noise was coming from somewhere along the boating lake, not far from where we were sitting. "A woman," I said, somewhat redundantly. No man could scream at such a high pitch and hold such a sustained note.

A group of ducks flew low across the surface of the lake, their shadows staining the water and their wings beating loudly. People ran towards the sound of the screams, excited by the potential for trouble. Chaos is always lurking just beneath the surface and, whenever it pops through to show itself, the crowds gather, sniffing for blood.

"Come on," said Mitch, caught up in the moment. "Let's check this out."

I glanced at my watch: 1:30 PM. We had half an hour before we were due back in our meeting, but the office was close enough that we could afford to humour Mitch's sense of curiosity. I followed him off the bench and along the shore of the lake, towards the slow-moving crowd which circled a patch of shoreline, where I could barely see what was happening – just a knot of onlookers and some kind of activity out in the water.

Only when we got close did I hear the voices.

"Come on, love, don't be silly. Get yourself back here. Nothing could be that bad." An old man wearing some kind of uniform – maybe that of St John's ambulance – was standing ankle-deep in the water with his trousers rolled up to his hairy knees. He was calling out to a young girl who was currently kneeling in the lake, perhaps a hundred yards away from his position. The girl had her back to him and she was staring up into the sky. She had on what appeared to be a school uniform – dark red blazer, white blouse, pleated grey skirt – and was holding her arms out from her body, almost in a crucifixion stance. That's what I remember most: her self-conscious, near-religious pose. Like a biblical martyr. I've seen that a few times since, but never as clear and unambiguous.

"Come on back ashore, love. Let's talk about this." The old man was inching forward, but trying not to get the cuffs of his trousers wet. He held one arm out, as if to offer her some kind of lifeline, and the other was pinned to his side.

"What the hell is this?" said Mitch, mostly to himself.

"Suicide bid," said a woman to my left. I looked over at her, and she pressed her lips together, as if trying to pretend that she hadn't spoken. Her curled hair was limp and moist; there was sweat on her brow.

"Really? What happened?"

The woman blinked at me before finally opening her lips. "Dunno. She just started putting rocks in her blazer pockets, and then walked out into the lake. We tried to stop her but... she didn't say a thing, just kept on walking out there. I think it's a cry for help."

I shook my head, more at the woman's TV-talk-show language than the situation, and then returned my gaze to the lake and the old man. And the girl. "Has anyone called the police?"

The woman didn't answer. Nor did anyone else. I made no move for my mobile phone, as if everyone else's reticence to inform the authorities had somehow taken hold of me, staying my hand. To this day, I still don't understand my lack of reaction to such an emergency.

The old man was now walking out towards the girl and muddy little eddies of water were sloshing around his thighs. He had gone deeper; his trousers were getting soaked. Somehow I doubted that he minded. I think he'd moved beyond such petty concerns, and now wanted only to help the girl.

He was still quite some distance from her, and narrowing the gap between them very slowly, so as not to spook her. She was facing the other way, but she must have been at least aware of his presence. It took me, and everyone around me, by surprise when she suddenly ducked her head beneath the surface of the water and kept it there.

"No!" It sounded as if we all shouted the same word at the same time: the force of the outcry was almost physical, punching a hole in the air.

The old man started to wave more vigorously, which prompted others from the shore to join him. They all splashed in there like excited dogs let off the leash. When the old man reached the girl he went down heavily beside her and struggled to drag her head up out of the water. The girl, or so it seemed from my vantage point, began to fight back. She kept her head under, throwing wild punches to the side, some of which connected with the old man. By the time the other would-be rescuers reached the spot, the girl was clawing at him.

It took four people to pull her out of the lake. They had to physically hold her above the surface as they carried her out, and when they laid her down at the side of the lake she jumped up and ran back into the water, throwing herself onto her belly in the shallows and pressing her face under the surface.

This happened three times, and in the end a heavyset man had to sit on her legs to prevent her from running again. She was breathless, puking up water, yet still she fought to be free. Her fists drummed against the ground and she wailed like a baby calling for food.

It turned out that someone had actually called the police. As we stood there watching, a siren approached and when I turned I saw a single police car driving across the grass towards us and then stop. The siren quieted and two uniformed officers got out of the vehicle. The crowd parted, forming a passage for the police to move through, and then rapidly closed again behind the officers.

Mitch and I watched in silence as the girl was handcuffed and escorted to the car. She still fought, craning her neck to look out across the lake, but by now she had tired considerably and her struggling was ineffectual. The water had settled down a bit, but a few ripples remained. I could tell that the girl still wanted nothing more than to drown herself in those waters.

We watched the police car depart, and then the crowd began to slowly disperse. The old man walked away, head down, refusing to make eye contact with anyone. People spoke in whispers, as if afraid to voice loudly their opinions on what we had all just witnessed. It made little sense and I felt the fear around me stirring the air. The sight of a young girl fighting to kill herself had unnerved everyone to the point that all theories were null and void. Whatever had just happened, it was truly inexplicable.

"Our meeting..." Mitch looked dazed, as if he'd just woken from a deep sleep. "We'd... we'd better go."

We walked in silence, neither of us able to even approach the subject; not right now, so close to the actual event. We left the park and crossed the road, staring up at the reflective glass windows of the office. Suddenly it looked daunting, as if brand new fears had been stirred by the scenes in the park – or perhaps ancient ones had resurfaced. Light burnished the glass, creating visions of another world – a place which had lurked somewhere unseen until now. A world that was suddenly, and slyly, encroaching upon our own.

CHAPTER 3

We entered the building, still not speaking. I felt detached, as if the shocking events in the park had jolted me out of my safe little bubble, in which I part-owned a successful architectural firm, had a wife who loved me and a baby on the way.

Sure, my wife was blind, but because she'd been that way since early childhood she knew how to navigate the world. It wasn't a big deal, just how she was. Her blindness was so much a part of her that I often forgot to tell people about the disability, and when finally they met her they were taken by surprise.

I was undeniably tethered to my existence and my problems were small ones; none of them were enough to even make me consider ending my own life. I wondered what had happened to the schoolgirl to make her think that there was no other way out than taking a long swim in shallow waters.

We walked across the building's main reception area and Mitch pressed the button to summon the elevator. I stared at the lift doors, at the gap where they didn't quite meet. Mitch was shifting his position, moving his feet on the plush carpeted floor. "What the hell did you make of that, then?"

I turned and looked at him. His face was pale; his lips looked thin and bloodless. "Honestly?"

Mitch nodded. I could sense that he was eager for someone to explain what we'd just seen – he was a realist, and needed plain facts to hang on to. It was how he survived, how he managed his life as well as our business.

"To be honest, I haven't a fucking clue. I'm trying to think of a situation to compare it to, but I'm coming up blank. I've... never seen anything like that. It was just crazy."

"So, that girl was mad? You think? She must've been." His eyes were wide, keen to pin a label on the girl's behaviour.

"Clearly," I said, not knowing either way if what we had seen was an example of mental problems reaching a crisis point or simply a sane reaction to an insane world. This latter thought bothered me. I wasn't usually so pessimistic, but recently my world had turned a shade darker than usual. The recession, all the projects being put on hold due to the global financial downturn. These worries were getting to me. I didn't even want to think about Kay's pregnancy, and how that had created worries I hadn't even been aware of six or seven months before.

The lift arrived, the doors sliding open to reveal an empty mirror-lined box. I let Mitch go in first and then followed him. He hit the button for the seventh floor and we waited as the lift rose quickly through the heart of the building. It stopped on the third and fifth floors, and a gorgeous young office girl got on at the latter. She was trim, blonde and had piercing blue eyes. Mitch smiled at her, but she blanked him. This served to take the edge off my mood – although it didn't quite work the same way for Mitch – and I was even grinning by the time we stepped out onto our floor. Such are the small ways in which other people's tragedies touch us, like a cool hand brushing against your cheek in the dark: strange and intense at the time, but soon forgotten.

We walked along the corridor, glancing into rooms and offices at people going through their normal routines, conducting the rites and rituals which made up the body of their day. Such common sights easily displaced the memory of the girl in the park, and I did not even pause to register the fact.

"Guys. You're late." Becky Talbot was walking towards us, smiling. Her long hair was pulled back into a tight ponytail and her crisp blue suit drew the eye in such a bland corporate environment. "We need to get back in there and finish the presentation. Gormley's been called away. Something about his wife."

Unconsciously, Mitch sidestepped to block Becky from my view. He always did that, tried to monopolise her attention. "What's wrong with his wife? She ill?" Mitch had been sleeping with Becky on and off for a couple of years, reanimating their never-quite-dead affair whenever he came to London on business.

Becky stopped and placed a hand on his arm. It was a small gesture, but said so much regarding how she felt about the man. It was both an indication of her affection and a way of warding him off before he got too close. "I'm not sure. I think she's been injured or something. An accident."

For some reason I thought again of the events in the park, and suddenly the office air conditioning felt too cold. It was an uncomfortable expression of the relationship between my surroundings and the horror I'd witnessed, forming a connection that I did not want to be aware of. I much preferred when I could compartmentalise the separate parts of my life, keeping barriers up and mental doors and windows firmly shut. Controlling how I felt about the world.

We followed Becky along the corridor to the meeting room, where the others were all waiting for us to continue outlining our concept design for the new mixed-use block – shops, offices and residential units – we'd been working on for months. If we were successful here, we stood the chance of making a lot of money on the job, more than enough to keep us afloat. The previous projects we'd worked on for the firm had all been small-scale; this was the biggest thing we'd ever tackled, and we felt confident that we could bring in a good design under budget.

"Sorry we're a bit late, gents," I said, moving towards the front of the room, where the digital projection screen formed a blank area which drew my eye. "There was some trouble in the park, and we got caught up in the crush."

I did not go into details, nor did anyone press me for further information. I was glad that I didn't have to go through it all again, even in my mind.

Morris and Turner were staring from their chairs, waiting for us to launch into action. Since the third and most senior partner in the development company – Gormley – was no longer on the premises they assumed joint command. I didn't like either of them, and Mitch could only stand them in small doses. Of the three, Gormley was the one we had forged a bond with over the past few years. The reality of his absence was that we would have to impress two old men who did not really like us.

The presentation went well, despite the personality conflicts, and we left the room feeling more confident than we'd expected. Morris had nodded a lot (which was always a good sign) and Turner had even cracked a smile when Mitch made a rather esoteric joke about the British Standards. We both had the feeling that we'd made up some good ground here, and that Gormley's empty seat had not been the big problem we'd expected. All in all, things looked promising.

"So," said Becky, approaching us afterwards in the main office, where I was drinking a cup of water from the dispenser and Mitch was adjusting the strap on his briefcase. "I hear it went well."

"Who said that? One of the old boys?" Mitch was suddenly alert: his political nature was a real asset to our company, while my strengths lay more in the technical side of things.

Becky nodded, moving closer to Mitch. Their bodies were almost touching. I could barely see daylight between them. "Turner was singing your praises. I overheard them when I went in there to get something signed."

Mitch smiled at me. He was a handsome man, and for a moment I felt sorry for his wife and experienced a visual echo of his many infidelities. If I looked behind him across the room, I imagined that I could see a long line of women standing in his wake, eyes downcast and hands wringing like those of mourners at a graveside.

"I think that's a good enough reason to get pissed this evening," he said, winking at me. "You up for that, Becky?" Of course she was; she always was. When Mitch called, she came running. I glanced at Mitch's hand. He wasn't wearing his wedding ring – never did. He said it cramped his style. In that moment, standing there with a plastic cup in my hand, I felt tempted to tell her that Mitch was married just to witness the fallout.

Becky rallied a few troops – the usual faces we drank with when we were here, each of them somehow similar, as if they had shared a mould. It was 4:30: early finishing on a Friday. A lot of the office staff lived outside London, and enjoyed going for an after-work drink until the rush hour was over and they could ride the trains back to their suburban flats and houses in peace. All they needed to convince them to stay out later was a reasonable excuse to celebrate.

"The first round's on us," said Mitch, and there went up a restrained roar of approval.

It was growing dim when we finally left the office. There was a small group of us – perhaps seven or eight in total – and we were heading towards The Wailing Well, a pub across the road we knew would still be quiet enough at this time of the day for us to grab a couple of tables and push them together. Mitch and Becky were in front of me. They were holding hands as they crossed the busy road. I was chatting with some IT guy called Tony and wishing I could break away or that it was time to call Kay. I telephoned her every evening when I was away, without fail. It was my ritual, and one that was as sacred to me as any religious act. Such concrete routines were yet another example of my constant need for control.

A couple of pints, I thought, and then I'll slip outside and call her on the mobile. She never went to bed until late, even now that she was pregnant, so I could afford to leave that for a while, but something inside me kept pressing me to make the call. I passed it off as anxiety caused by her pregnancy, but now I'm not so sure. If I did have any kind of insight at that point, it was lost in the traffic noise and the headlong rush towards the bar.

Mitch had somehow managed to isolate Becky from the rest of the group, and they were talking at the end of the bar, their hands clasped around the stems of wine glasses. Tony the IT guy handed me a pint of bitter before I could reach the bar to order anything and the rest of us retired to a table in the corner, next to a games machine and angled slightly into the large bay window. We shared small talk for a while and it turned out that one of the girls – a secretary called Hannah – had been present in the park at lunchtime, so the conversation turned to that topic. I didn't really want to talk about it again, but the subject seemed to grab everyone's attention.

Three or four pints later I was reaching for my mobile and thinking of calling Kay. It was now after 8pm. The place was filling up. There was a bunch of rugby types clustered at the back of the room, filling that area with noise, and various office workers had filtered in over the last couple of hours. People were piled two-deep at the bar; the bar staff were overworked and sweaty. I had lost sight of Mitch and Becky and didn't even know if they were still there or had sneaked off elsewhere to be alone.

There came a small lull or silence, as if a wedge of quietude had forced its way into the pub. The silence sat there, not really doing much but creating a sense of growing expectancy. Suddenly I decided to leave, to get outside and use my phone, call my wife. I was unsure where the urgency had sprung from, but it grabbed me by the throat and forced me to stand.

That's when things started to happen.

It began like a surge, or a wave of activity, pushing forward from the rear of the building. A glass shattered. Someone screamed. Heads turned. Eyes flashed. Something was happening – something potentially bad or dangerous – and we all wanted to see.

I was stuck in an awkward position, just rising from my chair, my arse suspended inches above the seat. I stared at my hand, where it rested on the table close to my almost empty glass, and then back at the room, at the customers all looking in the same direction.

An explosion of activity occurred somewhere off to the left, and two men emerged from the crowd. It looked at first as if they were dancing – arms wrapped around each other, feet moving in syncopation – but it soon became clear that they were locked in some kind of tussle. More glasses smashed. A few screams filled the air. Everyone moved back, away from the two men, as if this was part of an elaborately choreographed routine. There were no bouncers on duty: it wasn't that kind of place. That was why we came here, because of the easy atmosphere and the fact that there was never any trouble.

A few people took the opportunity to leave, blocking the door in their haste, but everyone else just stood and stared for a moment that stretched into two.

One of the men – the bigger of the two – managed to push the other away from him and kicked out at a table. The table tipped, spilling its contents all over the floor. Glass and liquid flooded the area at his feet.

The man's face. There was something wrong with it. The crowd surged away from him, sensing his otherness. His eyes were black, hard little stones pushed into the sockets. He was smiling. I realised that he was holding a bottle of whisky by the neck. As I watched, he lifted the bottle and tipped the whisky over his head. He waved the bottle as he poured, making sure that his head and shoulders and chest received a good covering of the fluid – an alcoholic baptism.

He was smiling.

The man then knelt down on the floor, his horrible black eyes staring at something none of the rest of us could see. In his other hand he produced a lighter. I didn't see where he got it from. One minute his hand was empty, the next he was flicking the lighter, trying to summon a spark.

A small flame leapt from his fist. The flame looked huge in the panicked room.

He was smiling.

The way to the door was fully blocked by now; almost everyone was trying to leave, to push their way out onto the street. The head barman vaulted over the bar and rushed towards the kneeling man, his arms outstretched and his face a smudged white patch against the high, dark walls.

The man on the floor moved the lighter flame towards his face.

He was smiling.

The flame caught, setting light to his hair: the whisky aided combustion and within seconds his whole head was aflame, then his shoulders, and finally his torso.

He was smiling.

By the time the barman reached the man there was nothing he could do. The air filled with the stench of burning cloth and charring flesh; thick black greasy smoke rose towards the ceiling, staining the plaster. The flaming man did not move; he was still smiling.

I scrambled out of my chair and headed for the door, pushing people out of my way. Smoke and screams filled the pub, and then I heard the sound of a fire extinguisher being used. *Too late,* I thought. *It's all too late.*

Outside, standing at the kerb and waiting for the sirens, watching women weep and men stare emptily into the road, I calmly took out my mobile and called Kay.

CHAPTER 4

— *It's me*

— *How are you, baby?*

— *Not good. Something's just happened in the pub. The whole city's gone crazy.*

— *Really?*

— *Yes. It's weird. I've seen two people try to kill themselves today — it's like some kind of suicide cult.*

— *Bloody hell. I heard something on the news today, about two girls trying to throw themselves under cars on the M25. I wonder if it's the same thing.*

— *I dunno. Don't care. How's He-She? Any kicking today?*

— *Both He-She and I miss you loads, and, yes, there's been some kicking. Plenty of kicking.*

— *Miss you more. Hopefully I'll be back home by this time tomorrow. One last meeting with our potential contractor in the morning, and then we're through.*

— *Are things going well?*

— *I think so. I hope so. They seem impressed.*

— *They should be. You're an impressive man.*

— *I know.*

— *Cheeky.*

— *I love you, you know.*

— *I know you do. And we love you. Hurry back, and bring good news.*

— *I will. Mitch says hello, by the way.*

— *Tell him we both say hello back.*

— *Send He-She kisses from me.*

— *Right back at you.*

— *See you soon.*

— *You'd better.*

CHAPTER 5

I stood outside The Wailing Well with everyone else, stuck in a kind of limbo. A few people had moved away, crossing the road and heading for other drinking holes, but the majority of the pub's customers were milling around on the pavement outside waiting for someone to tell them what to do. It was as if the massive violence of what we'd all witnessed had taken away our sense of individuality and we were looking for a leader.

Mitch and Becky came towards me from the other end of the building. Mitch had his hands in his pockets and Becky was pale and quiet. "What the fuck's going on, Mack?"

I shook my head: I wasn't the leader they were looking for. "I know as much as you do, mate. That bloke went mental."

There was a slight commotion when the barman who'd taken charge came out of the pub, holding a fire extinguisher. His hair was in disarray and his shirt had come undone, several buttons having popped off in the commotion. He looked shell-shocked, like someone walking out of a demolished building after being trapped inside when the walls came down. A woman put her arm around his shoulders and he began to weep quietly.

"Something's wrong," I said, still staring at the crumbling barman.

"You don't say." Mitch stepped close to me. One of his hands came out of his pocket and he lightly touched my arm. "You okay?"

I turned to face him. He looked tired. They all did, every single bystander gathered around us on the pavement. I probably looked the same. "Yeah. What I mean is, there's something *very* wrong. Not just here, tonight, but maybe in general. Remember that girl earlier, in the park? I spoke to Kay a few minutes ago and she told me about two women throwing themselves under cars on the motorway. It isn't right; none of it."

Becky lit a cigarette and sucked deeply, the tip glowing like a tiny beacon in the darkness. "There's been other stuff, too. I saw on a news website at lunch that a lot of suicides had been reported... an 'unusual number', or so they said." Her hand shook as she placed the filtered end to her lips. Smoke curled around her narrow, pretty features.

Gary McMahon

"Fucking hell!" It was a man's voice, quite close to us outside the pub. We all turned, and saw a thin man in a brown leather jacket and torn jeans sitting with his back against the wall. He had an open laptop on the ground between his legs, and he was staring at the screen. His legs and lower body were bathed in unearthly light. He had small headphones in his ears, and the wire terminated at a connection port in the side of his machine. "Look at this."

Those nearest the man gathered in close, trying to catch a glimpse of the laptop screen. I managed to get myself into a position to see what he was looking at so intently, but it took me several seconds to understand the significance of what was playing out on the screen. Then, realisation: part of the appeal of The Wailing Well, and why it had a steady clientele, was that the owner had shelled out for free wifi internet access. Clearly this man, whoever he was, was still connected to the web.

"What is it? This isn't real. Tell me it's not real." This from a woman, smartly dressed in a pinstripe business suit. She was holding her hands against her cheeks, as if trying to squeeze her face thin.

On the screen there was a report from the BBC News website. I could not hear what was being said, but the images were clear enough. Playing in a loop, inter-cut with talking heads back in the studio, was amateur footage taken outside Number 10 Downing Street less than an hour ago. Depicted in shaky hand-held pictures, one of the policemen who stood on guard outside the Prime Minister's permanent residence took his revolver from inside his jacket, placed it against his temple, and blew his brains out. It happened fast; the whole thing took no more than a few seconds. Gun out. Put barrel to head. Pull trigger. Red spray.

"They're saying things like this are happening all over London." The owner of the laptop was finally speaking, but I wished that he'd just shut the fuck up. I didn't want to hear; it was too insane to take in. "People are killing themselves, like some kind of mass hysteria. The police are advising that everyone should stay indoors. Go home and lock yourself in until everything's under control."

Mitch pressed against me. I turned to face him and saw that his eyes were wide and dark and filled with what I could only assume was horror. I didn't know, wasn't sure: before then, I had never seen real horror in a person's face. Now I have seen too much of it. Way too much.

"Just stay calm," I said, but I wasn't sure who I was trying to reassure. "This can't be true. It's just a coincidence." I did not even believe my own words.

"What should we do?" Becky was lighting another cigarette, but her hands shook so much that she dropped it on the ground. "Shit." She did not bend to pick it up: her eyes were glued to the laptop. "What the hell do we do?"

I looked out at the road, wondering where the sirens were. It seemed as if we'd been out here for ages, standing at the kerb, and no emergency services had arrived. I could hear muted sirens in the distance, of course – too many of them, now that I thought about it – but none of them were getting any closer. "Let's just get back to our hotel. We can discuss things calmly there, over a few stiff drinks."

Mitch took a step backwards, away from the man with the laptop, as if he'd simply been waiting for the opportunity to do so. "Yeah. Good idea. Let's go. I've had enough of this shit." I had never seen him so afraid.

We left the crowd outside The Wailing Well, and when I looked back I saw Tony the IT guy standing in the road, speaking animatedly into a mobile phone. If he was calling a taxi, he might have to wait a while. Somehow I didn't think that the normal urban services would be operating at their best this evening. The sirens remained distant, taunting us from another part of the city – probably Central London, somewhere near Downing Street – and I wished that I was back home, up north, sitting watching all this on the evening news and holding Kay's small, cold hand. Her hands were always cold, since she'd fallen pregnant. It was one of the things we laughed about.

"This way," I said, taking the lead. If I took control, it might stop me from thinking about Kay and the baby – the unborn baby we called He-She. That was another thing we laughed about.

I wanted to laugh now; I wanted this so badly that it hurt. But I couldn't; laughter was not a normal, sane response to what was happening here. Whatever *was* happening here…because that was the real question wasn't it? But I doubted that anyone had a realistic answer.

The three of us headed away from Baker Street, towards Lord's cricket ground. One of the floodlights was on, but the rest were dark. I hadn't been told of anything going on there, a corporate event or night match, so assumed that the caretaker was doing an inspection or some late night work on the pitch.

We were leaving the Congestion Charge Zone, so traffic became heavier the farther we moved from its perimeter. It might have been my imagination, but it seemed to me that each vehicle that passed us was going slightly too fast, their drivers keen to get wherever they were going. I suspected that there would be a lot of accidents, and not all of them caused by suicides.

There, I'd admitted it: the truth of the situation. I pushed the thought away, trying not to dwell on it.

"Come on, keep up." No one was lagging behind, but as usual I felt the need to impose some kind of control. I led them along the edge of the park in the direction of St John's Wood. Our hotel was near the tube station, a cheap, nondescript place that we always used whenever we had business in the City – one of those generic HumBird Inns you used to see everywhere back then. Mitch had discovered the hotel a few years before, when he had visited it with some old girlfriend he'd hooked up with through an internet networking site. The rendezvous had been a bad idea, but the rooms were clean and the hotel staff very discreet when it came to the paperwork. Mitch's wife had never found out.

When I looked at him now, scurrying along behind me, holding Becky's hand, I wondered how he could be such a bastard to the person who loved him most and such a good guy with everyone else.

We were now mere yards from the hotel, almost running just to get there. A car mounted the kerb opposite, clipping the wall, and when I looked at the driver I saw that he was crying. The car pulled away, turning a corner and vanishing from sight. I heard what sounded like the soft *whump* of impact, as if the car had collided with a body, but kept on driving, not wanting to get involved. My mind was telling me that someone had thrown themselves into the path of the car, but my body wasn't prepared to investigate. The sirens sounded even more distant. Streetlights flickered but remained lit. I took it as a sign that the city was rapidly going into meltdown.

The HumBird Inn looked quiet, yet the lights were on in most of the rooms, and the light from the downstairs bar spilled out through the windows in a wide aura. We entered the building and walked past the empty reception desk. Even from there we could hear the television in the bar – someone had turned the volume up, and the news was on.

I glanced at the other two, and they both indicated that we should head in that direction rather than going straight up to our rooms. It seemed like the hub of the building and offered warmth and light and companionship.

The bar area was busier than I had seen it since we checked in the day before. It looked as if almost everyone staying in the hotel was crammed into the room, yet most of them were silent. Couples and businessmen on their own, a few families, and an old man in the corner staring at the television screen. In fact, everyone there was watching the television, their eyes flat and shining like new coins reflecting the light from the screen.

A young girl stood behind the bar. I'd seen her before, earlier that morning when she was serving breakfast. I nodded at her. She moved to the edge of the bar as we approached. The television news was reporting more suicides – teenage joyriders driving into an abutment of the Blackwall Tunnel, people jumping out of windows at the Barbican Estate, a family of squatters somehow setting fire to an entire street in Camden. These things were happening all over the city, not just in the vicinity of the initial reports. It was spreading, fanning out like a virus moving inexorably through a healthy body.

"What can I get you?" The girl's face was drawn; she looked tired. Her hair was short and blonde and she had a red gemstone piercing her left nostril. Her eyes were the palest blue I had ever seen, like cornflowers. "Three whiskies, please. Doubles." I did not even consult my companions. We needed strong drinks, and I doubted that either of them would complain.

"Let's go over here." Mitch guided Becky across the room towards one of the only free tables, which was located in the farthest corner from the wall-mounted television. I waited for our drinks, paid, and then followed. We all took a sip in silence, as if we were afraid to voice the reality of the situation. Unspoken, this could all be passed off as some kind of fiction, but if we opened our mouths and uttered anything the events might become solid facts.

I watched the television, my head beginning to ache yet my vision taking on a peculiar kind of clarity. Talking heads in a London studio; frightened people interviewed in a fire-lit street; endless static shots of police cars, ambulances and fire engines making their way through the city.

"I'm not sure if I fucking believe this." Becky was entranced; her hand was held up near her mouth, as if she did not want the glass to stray too far from her lips. Her smooth cheeks were bloodless and her brown eyes looked huge, the pupils dilated. "It's too crazy to be real."

Mitch reached across the table and grasped her arm, but she showed no sign of even noticing the gesture. She looked numb, inside and out, and I feared for a moment that she might enter a state of shock, her mind simply shutting out the impossibility of what was happening. But she took another drink, swallowed hard, and regained her focus. "We need to do something. We need to help, or something. All of us."

I knew exactly what Becky meant; she was not referring to us three, gathered around the little table, or even the rest of the people in the bar. She meant everyone, the entire populace. We all needed to help, if we could. Aid was required, and the emergency services seemed stretched beyond their capacity to cope.

As if in answer, a message began to scroll across the bottom of the television screen, an echo of the advice we had heard already: *London residents are advised to stay in their homes. Lock the doors. Secure the property. Do not leave your homes.* The message scrolled in an endless band, as if Becky's plea for assertive action had prompted its appearance.

"I think we should do what they say." I put my glass on the table, but kept my fist wrapped tightly around it. "I mean, if people start flooding the streets in some uncoordinated effort to help, it can only make things worse. Let's just stay here – Becky, you can stay with us."

"I know. You're right. I… I was just trying to get my head around this whole thing. Let's hope things are better in the morning." She smiled at me; then she looked across at Mitch, who was still holding on to her arm. "I'll stay here with you."

I thought of Kay, and hoped that she was okay. She was miles away from this, safe and sound in the Yorkshire countryside, but still I feared for her safety. This could just be the start of things, an initial outbreak of a mutant strain of paranoia that might spread across the country, causing people to kill themselves.

Glancing at the windows, I saw darkness writhing outside. It looked alive, sentient, as if it were an animal prowling for prey. The room felt warm and tiny; the people in here with me began to seem like a crowd, a mob-in-waiting. I was tired, my limbs were heavy. The television droned in the background, subsumed by the sudden chattering voices inside the bar.

I closed my eyes and prayed that when I opened them everything would be normal.

It wasn't.

CHAPTER 6

After a few more drinks we went upstairs to our rooms, none of us speaking much as we rode in the lift. The silence lengthened. It stretched between us and became almost tangible as we stepped out onto the third floor landing and trod the length of the corridor, three weary people in need of rest. Mitch and Becky were still holding hands. It was as if they were clinging to something that neither of them could quite define, but they both knew that if they let go they might lose it forever.

I stopped at my door, letting them walk on a pace or two before coming to a halt at the one next to mine. "See you in the morning."

Becky nodded.

"Do you think we should still go to the meeting?" Mitch's voice sounded tiny, like that of a child. "I mean, will anyone be going into the office?" I'd never known him sound so vulnerable.

"I say we go in there, see what's what, and then try to get things packed up so we can get out of the city as soon as possible. I have a feeling a lot of people will be calling in sick in the morning, or absent on compassionate leave… things should be quiet. I only hope the trains are still running."

"Fuck. I never thought of that," said Becky. "Shit. If those news reports are anything like accurate, a lot of people have killed themselves over the last twenty-four hours. That means the services will be down to a minimum. I don't mean to sound heartless or anything, but things might come to a standstill."

We all stood in silence for a moment, letting that one sink in.

"Shit," said Mitch. "You don't think of that stuff at the time, do you? I mean, when everything's happening. You just deal with the moment."

"Let's just go to bed. We all need some rest." I took out my plastic key-card and slipped it into the slot in the door. The green light came on after a second or two of jiggling, and the mechanism unlocked the door. "We'll meet downstairs at eight."

"Yeah." Mitch opened his own door and went inside.

"See you then." Becky flashed me a nervous smile – one that

seemed to be hiding what looked to me like guilt – and followed him, closing the door behind her.

Once I was inside my own room, I could hear the muffled sound of their voices through the wall. I couldn't make out what they were saying, but I did hear my name mentioned a couple of times. They both sounded scared – Becky more so, and I imagined Mitch doing his best to calm her down. He was good at that: calming people down, smoothing out the edges. I always said he should have been a salesman not an architect.

I turned on the television simply to shut out the sound of them talking, and watched a repeat of the same news reports I'd already seen in the bar downstairs. Things seemed to be tailing off; the city was in chaos, but no new suicides had been reported for the last half hour. The authorities were stretched to the limits of their resources trying to clean up the mess.

My stomach growled, demonstrating the first signs of hunger since lunchtime. I stared at the phone on the nightstand, but knew that I wouldn't pick it up. I only ever called Kay once in the evening, and never after bedtime. She needed ritual and routine as much as I did, especially now that she was pregnant, and any break from our usual habits might send her into a panic and make her believe that I was in trouble. I looked at my watch: half past midnight. She would be asleep now, anyway, feeding the baby with her dreams.

And what dreams she had – every one of them a show of strength. Kay had been blinded in an accident when she was nine years old. Walking the few yards home from the corner shop in the rain one day, she had crossed the road without looking, caught up in a conversation with her friend. The friend had almost seen the car – a stolen Ford Sierra – in time, and grabbed Kay's shoulder with the intention of pulling her back onto the kerb. If the Sierra had been travelling at or below the speed limit, both girls might have got away with minor injuries, but because it was moving at speed (the police later estimated this at 60 mph in a 30 mph zone) Kay's friend had been knocked off her feet, and flew backwards towards the shops behind, her body shattering the display window of a clothing boutique.

The teenage boy driving the car died in the crash. His younger passenger suffered internal bleeding but lived. Both of them had been high on smack. Kay's friend never walked again, and Kay had been blind since the moment the car hit her.

We met when she was sixteen and I was seventeen. Kay was on the verge of leaving school after her exams and it was my first year of University. I had been out with friends at Bradford ice rink and seen a girl holding on to the wooden barrier, afraid to leave its protection. I only saw her from behind, but I knew without seeing her face that she was beautiful.

Feeling brash because I was with my mates, I skated over and started chatting her up. Only when she turned to me did I see that she was wearing dark glasses, but it still didn't dawn upon me that she couldn't see. I just thought that she was pretty vain, wearing sunglasses indoors. Maybe she thought she was a rock star. In retrospect, ice-skating was a typical Kay thing to do.

We arranged to meet for a coke in the café after our session, and the first thing she said to me when I saw her at the table, approached and sat down was, "I'm blind, you know." Her forthright statement won me over from the start, and despite the mockery of my friends I realised that I was lost.

Her parents were dubious at first, wondering what such a popular young man wanted with their blind daughter. It took me weeks to convince them that my intentions were true, but once they trusted me they welcomed me into their home and soon began to treat me like one of the family.

That was exactly what I needed at the time. My own family, or what was left of it, resembled a war zone. My father had died from a sudden coronary when I was eight, leaving my mother bitter and drink-addicted. Whenever she even noticed me, she would stare at me with a look of such loathing that it twisted my insides to witness her features. I looked like my dad, and she simply couldn't handle that. Instead of coming to terms with his death, she resented the fact that he had left her alone. Then she started to resent me for being his double.

So I took refuge in Kay's family, and she took solace from me. I had learned to be strong; my reputation around my home town was that of a tough guy. I had been fighting for as long as I could remember – fighting the absence my father had left behind and fighting the fact that my mother hated me. What was a simple playground fist fight compared to subtle and ceaselessly damaging battles such as these?

I protected Kay. If anyone as much as smiled at her the wrong way (or what I deemed as being the wrong way) I hit them and I hit them hard. I created a bubble around us, and for the time being this fitted Kay's needs.

My father had taken out a substantial insurance policy, and just to get rid of me my mother used some of it to fund my education. I had always loved buildings, and been fascinated by the process of construction (rather than the destruction I saw all around me) ever since I could remember.

That insurance money was the only reason I was able to study architecture, and during seven years at university I was glad of the regular income and the fact that my bills were taken care of. I moved out of my mother's house to rent a small flat in Leeds, and Kay moved in with me. My father's money meant that I didn't have to share a grotty place with other students. She studied psychology with a view to becoming a social worker (unsurprisingly, she wanted to help blind kids adjust to the world). Things were great back then and, when she qualified and took a job with the local council, they got even better. My small fund combined with Kay's salary meant that we were comfortable, at least as far as our relatively small-scale needs were concerned.

We worked hard, earning whatever small success came our way. By the time we married, my mother was dead from sclerosis of the liver. I never missed her for even a moment. Kay's dad gave her away, and my best man was a guy called Mitch who I'd met during my first year of studies.

Lying on the stiff hotel bed, my eyes began to tear up; the moisture blurred my vision, and for a moment I thought that I might be overcome by this strange, nameless emotion. The television droned in the background; occasional car headlights splashed the room with smeared pools of illumination; the walls closed in, becoming soft and enveloping.

I was aware that I was dreaming, but that didn't make the images any less confusing. I was running through an empty street, the houses on either side of me supple, as if they were made of flesh and bone not brick and mortar. Walls swayed, windows undulated, doors flickered open and closed like heavy eyelids. The architecture was foreign to my eye – perhaps even alien. Never before had I seen such shapes applied to a building structure.

Someone was chasing me, but I had no idea who (or what) it was. There was the *notion* of pursuit; a sensation that I was being followed, but no sounds to back it up. I kept running, too afraid to stop and test if there was indeed any pursuer behind me. Approaching a dark area where there were no houses – just an empty patch of land between two weird buildings – I glanced sideways and saw something stirring within the layers of darkness. It was as if an animal were shifting, or perhaps a *group* of animals; I saw a faint fluttering motion, and heard what sounded like feet or paws padding towards me across the rubble.

Suddenly I knew that whatever had been chasing me had caught up, and that it was squatting in the dark alongside me, waiting for me to enter its domain. That same nightmare certainty told me that the thing would not pounce; it would wait. And it possessed an infinite patience.

When I woke up I was confused; I didn't know where I was. I reached out a hand across the mattress, expecting it to come into contact with my wife, but when I realised the bed was empty reality began to once again impose itself on the moment.

I sat up, blinking into the dark, and saw that same presence from my dream kneeling in the corner. It was without shape; just a blur of blackness against the wall, and again I was struck by the fact that it was waiting. Biding its time. The choice, it seemed, was mine: either ignore it or run headlong into a violent confrontation.

I blinked, and it was gone. But it was still there – *always* there, in the darkness behind my eyes. More than the clinging residue of a recurring nightmare, it was a solid presence in my life, a thing to which I had grown accustomed, but whose power I never underestimated. It was the echo of my own mortality, as well as those of my wife and unborn child.

It was Death, pure and simple.

Restless and unable to get back to sleep, I stood up and went to the mini bar. I took out a Smirnoff miniature, twisting off the top and pouring the contents into a glass. There was no ice, so it tasted harsh; but I liked its honesty.

I was still wearing my clothes – the bed had called to me before I had the chance to undress. I loosened my tie, then took it off and threw it onto the chair. Taking a long gulp of the vodka, I closed my eyes and tried to inhale the calmness of the room. After a few moments of stillness, I began to undress. Then I sat like a slob in my underwear, perched on the end of the mattress and sipping my drink. The television bled dead light onto my bare legs; the images capering across the screen no longer meant anything to me.

I finished my drink and placed the glass on the floor. Then, feeling slightly less tense, I lay back on the bed, my legs dangling over the edge, and waited for sleep to once again claim me. It was a long time coming, but eventually it dragged me away.

I went with it, but I went screaming. Screaming inside.

CHAPTER 7

The television was still on when I woke the next morning. The news reporters were still covering yesterday's events with wide-eyed glee and an obscene hint of anticipation. They wanted more deaths – the more spectacular the better – to ensure continued good ratings figures. It was a depressing indictment of modern reportage, but I suppose we get the culture we ask for. I remembered an old adage from my schooldays, something about the notion that any society should be judged by its prisons. I disagreed: society should always be judged by its morning news reports.

The official advice to lock oneself indoors had been abandoned, and it looked as if the authorities were now trying to act as if everything was back to normal: just another day in the big city. Please ignore the dead people in the gutters as you make your way to work this morning.

"Fuck off," I muttered, swinging my legs off the bed as I slapped the remote control in order to silence the inane chatter. I walked through into the bathroom and took a shower, then cleaned my teeth to get rid of the stale aftertaste of last night's alcohol. I had to clean them twice to remove the greasy film that had covered the enamel overnight.

I dressed slowly in the silent room, wishing that I was at home. Despite the reports that things seemed to be calming down, I was filled with a sense of impending dread. I picked up my mobile phone and saw that I had a text message from Kay.

Love you. Miss you. xxx

We had paid a lot of money for a specially designed mobile phone with voice recognition and a speech synthesiser, and it meant that she could keep in touch with me via texts whenever she wanted. It was tricky to use, but Kay had quickly grown accustomed to the somewhat clumsy procedure. She taught Braille at a local college twice a week; a smart woman, my wife…much more intelligent than me.

I replied to her message, so that she knew everything was fine. Deep down, though, I still felt uneasy because we were such a great distance apart. We are all given a false sense of distance by modern communication technologies, but a mile is still a mile and there were far too many of them between my wife and me. If anything was to go wrong, and she needed me quickly, it was such a long way to run…

It was 8:30 a.m. Time to go. I finished packing my things and grabbed my coat, then left the room and stood outside the next door along on the quiet landing, hoping that by knocking I wouldn't interrupt any early-morning intimacy between Mitch and Becky.

I knocked twice and the door opened.

"Come in. Won't be a minute." Mitch looked rather pale, but he was at least smiling. His shirt was unbuttoned to the navel but he was otherwise presentable. "Becky's just doing her hair." He nodded towards the bathroom as he walked across to the window, tucking his shirt into his trousers and doing up the buttons.

Outside the sun was struggling to beat back the morning dimness. Thin spears of sunlight pierced the clouds, adding subtle shades to the new day. I stared at the sky, entranced by the slow interplay of light and darkness, barely aware of the bathroom door opening behind me.

"Morning, Mack. How did you sleep?"

I turned around, jolted out of my little reverie. Becky looked smart and sexy in her miraculously uncreased suit, her hair brushed and her make-up neatly applied. She was ready for business. She must have skilfully employed the room's trouser press – a gadget I had never once even thought of using in all my years staying in hotels. "Not bad, I suppose. Under the circumstances."

She grimaced, her face twisting as if she'd eaten something nasty. "I know. Me too." She glanced at Mitch; her face coloured slightly. That single look told me that neither of them had slept much last night. I couldn't blame them. If Kay had been with me, I'd have sought the comfort of sex, too.

We took the lift downstairs, talking about anything except the events of the previous day. We were all delicately manoeuvring around the subject, frightened to touch what had happened in case it tried to bite us like a wounded animal. It was there, we all knew that was, but we had tacitly decided to leave well alone for the time being.

There were not many people up and about this morning. Bob something-or-other, the hotel's manager, passed us in the hall, nodding and wishing us good morning. He seemed distracted; his eyes evaded us. I wondered if he had lost someone. I knew he had an ex-wife somewhere, but had never heard him speak of her other than in passing. I didn't know him well enough to ask after his family's welfare. This made me aware of how little we actually know the people we come into contact with, even those we see regularly.

After grabbing some coffee and toast, we walked to the office, past slow-moving city-bound traffic and pedestrians walking at a much more casual pace than usual. There were fewer commuters on the streets than there should have been, as if a lot of them had decided to stay at home rather than make the journey into work. I understood that. I was only out and about because I had no choice – because I was here, and having to attend stupid fucking meetings, rather than at home where I belonged. A dark and confusing rage threatened to rise up and spill out of me, but I held it back. Now was not the time for mindless reactions.

The pavements were covered in litter – fast food wrappers, crisp packets, crushed beer cans and broken bottles. The gutters were blocked with detritus. Amazing how filthy a city can become in one night.

I spotted an army vehicle turning the corner towards Baker Street, a small all-terrain truck with several squaddies hanging off the sides. Then, as if the first sight had been a cue of some kind, four armed policemen strolled around the same corner, but moving towards us. They weren't walking with any kind of conviction, but there was a deliberation to their slow, regular strides that made me realise they were not simply out for a morning stroll.

"Fucking hell." Mitch stopped, grabbing Becky's arm to hold her back. "This is some serious shit."

I stared at the uniformed officers. They had automatic weapons slung over their shoulders and were wearing stab vests and riot helmets with protective plastic visors. The visors were in the up position – which meant that the officers must be relatively relaxed and not expecting any immediate trouble, but it was a sobering sight all the same.

A bus with no passengers moved slowly along the road, stopping by the park. The driver just sat there, talking into his radio. Then, as if he'd been waiting for a signal, he reached up and switched the sign above the windscreen to read "Out of Service". A few moments later the bus was chugging past us, the driver's unshaved face staring straight ahead.

"Should we even bother with this?" I turned to the others, unable to make up my own mind. "I mean, will anyone even bother to turn up for work?"

Becky nodded. "I rang before we left. There aren't many people due in – some of them lost family last night and others are simply taking holiday or a sickie – but a couple of the directors made it in early, along with a few hard-core career arse-kissers."

"Don't tell me," I said. "Morris and Turner arrived at the crack of dawn, didn't they?"

Becky was almost smiling. "Yeah, they're like fucking machines. They've never missed a day in over thirty years. Turner even came in when his wife died of cancer last spring. He threatened to fire anyone who as much as suggested that he take compassionate leave. When we gave him a condolence card he didn't put it up or even make a comment."

I wondered how the third director – Gormley – was doing. He was the only one of the trio I liked; he'd been good to Mitch and me over the years, recommending us for jobs and letting us in on hush-hush tenders, some of which had led to lucrative contracts in the south. I hoped the old guy was okay, and that his wife had not been one of last night's many victims...

"Come on," said Mitch. "Let's get off the street before the police ask us what we're doing. I have a feeling anyone out and about today is going to get some shit from that lot." Mitch had never trusted the authorities, and even went out of his way to be unhelpful if he happened to be involved in a situation with the police. I knew his distrust of authority went back to childhood, when a close friend of his had been killed by a police vehicle in pursuit of a criminal. I knew little more than those few basic facts, but the event had clearly left Mitch with deep mental scars. I suspected he'd been a witness to what had happened, despite him never having let on as much. I'd never pushed him to tell me about it. Mitch had depths that even I hadn't plumbed.

We entered the building and climbed the stairs. For some reason none of us had made a move towards the lift, nor did we mention why that might be.

The office was more than half empty. A few familiar faces sat at desks, pretending to work or whispering to each other and glancing suspiciously about the room. The atmosphere was horrible, filled with tension and a sort of unwelcome sense of anticipation. I wanted to leave, right away, but if the directors were acting as if it was business as usual we needed to go along with their routine if we still held out any hope of winning that job.

"You two sit there and make yourself comfortable. Grab a coffee or something. I'll go and see how the land lies." Becky moved away, smiling wanly at Mitch. He winked at her and her cheeks coloured a subtle shade of pink. She often blushed in his presence. *Fuck off,* she mouthed silently as she whisked away.

I realised in that moment that their fling meant more to her than just casual sex. Becky was in love with Mitch, and if he even realised the depth of her feelings he certainly was not able to reciprocate them.

"Do you think we'll be able to get an earlier train? I very much doubt anything of substance is going to happen here today. We might as well count our blessings and skedaddle."

Mitch looked at me. His eyes were heavy-lidded. "Skedaddle? How old are you, seventy? And do you even think the trains are running, Granddad?"

"Surely… I mean, there are people here, at work. The trains *must* be running."

"Maybe they were early this morning, or these people all just drove in – the roads will have been pretty empty, I guess. But when we saw those armed police out there it got me thinking that things might be on some kind of semi-lockdown. I dunno. Maybe I'm full of shit, but I don't have a very good feeling right now."

I shook my head. "I don't think anyone has a good feeling about any of this, mate. The only positive I can see is that whatever happened last night seems to have stopped. I think those armed police are just mopping up the mess, and keeping an eye out in case it starts up again."

"Yeah." Mitch lowered his head, ran his hands through his hair. "Yeah. You're right. It's over. Let's just get this crap out of the way and head for the station. Get home. Forget about last night." When he looked back up his face was pale, his lips a tight slash above his chin. He looked terrified.

Becky's footsteps brought us back into the moment, making us both look up and along the corridor. "You're not going to believe this, but those two old twats want to continue the meeting. They told me that the only way to deal with a situation like this is to keep on going, act like nothing has happened." She was shaking her head and seemed poised on the verge of laughter. "Unbelievable."

"Fucking hell. If I saw this in a film, I'd turn the thing off." Mitch stood up, smoothing his trouser legs. "I'm game if you are. Shall we?"

I slowly got to my feet and we headed towards the meeting room, with Becky trailing us, her steps brisk and efficient – just like always.

It's amazing how we slip back into the familiar routines after something monumental has happened, especially if it hasn't affected us directly. I doubted that Gormley, or any of his staff who had lost people last night, would be so eager to resume their usual daily roles, to try and keep the wheels of commerce moving. But that's exactly what we did.

"Ah, gentlemen… So glad you could rejoin us today." Turner stood from behind the table, his big belly wobbling as he moved. "Becky, could you rustle us up some coffee?" He actually used those words: *rustle us up some coffee*. I felt like smacking him in the mouth, just to shock him into some kind of reaction.

Morris, the skinny half of this double act, remained seated, but nodded his head like one of those stupid dashboard dogs. His wig was immaculate, but his suit looked creased and slightly grubby.

Mitch went to the drawer where we'd stashed some of our papers and sketches, and I took the rest from my briefcase. The screen was still connected to the laptop from yesterday, so I just turned on the power and checked that everything was still working as it should be.

Then we launched into our second presentation – the one we hoped would win us the contract. We both believed that the preliminary brief was good enough to warrant a contract, and as we got into our rhythm it became apparent that our audience was beginning to feel the same.

It happened near the end of the presentation, when the two directors were already won over. They were both smiling – a rarity; it was considered an astonishing feat to please them both at the same time – and Mitch was bantering like a stand-up comic on the last night of a tour.

I hadn't said much, preferring to work the technology and hand out sketches. Mitch's strength was in the boardroom, while mine was in the design office. I felt more comfortable with a set-square in my hand than I did with a smarmy quip between my lips.

Mitch was in mid-flow, pacing before his captive audience and waving his hands about in front of him as he described some nuance of the design. He was facing the room, with his back to the window, so didn't see the first black shape as it fell.

"What was that?" Turner's chins vibrated; his piggy eyes widened. "What…" Before he finished repeating the question, another blurred shape plummeted past the window.

I stood and stared, realising immediately what I was seeing, yet barely able to believe it. Men in business suits were falling past the window, heading for the pavement.

As I stared, another three or four went past. This time one of them clipped against the window, splintering the glass. Another. Then another. They looked like giant bats swooping past the window, wings flapping madly as they dived to the ground.

"Fucking hell…" Mitch was backing away, his hands reaching behind him for the table he knew was there somewhere. His left hand knocked the laptop, tipping it off its stand, and just as I was about to shout a warning Turner stood and launched himself across the table.

It was an astonishing sight: a man weighing at least twenty stones leaping across a varnished desk, his shiny shoes sliding, his big belly swaying. He slammed into Mitch as he made for the window, and somehow his arm linked through Mitch's elbow as he charged across the carpet.

Both men went barrelling forward, Mitch almost spinning as he was pulled away from the table, and the big man moving fast, with his head down: a bull calmly charging towards its death.

It was over in an instant. One minute they were both there, standing in the office; the next the window was completely broken, cold air was billowing inside, and Mitch and Turner had gone through the jagged hole. I assumed it was Mitch screaming all the way down while Turner remained silent. The screaming didn't last long, not really, but it felt like an eternity. I can still hear it now, whenever I close my eyes: it feels like it never really stopped.

I stared for a moment that felt like hours, and then, finally, I managed to drag my gaze from the broken window and look back at the table. Morris was still sitting there, in his rumpled suit and his tidy little hairpiece. His neck was still bleeding where he'd opened it with a fountain pen, stabbing the metal tip across his throat. His black eyes were open and his mouth was closed. He must have done the deed in silence. That was what scared me most, and what finally got my legs moving so that I could run out of the meeting room to look for help.

CHAPTER 8

Help wasn't something that was readily available right then. If there was any in the vicinity, it was either hiding in a cupboard or otherwise engaged. I ran right into Becky, who was coming the other way. Her blouse was untucked from her trousers and she was breathing heavily.

"Don't," I said, positioning myself so that my body was between her and the door to the room I'd just left. "Come on, we need to get out of here." I was acting on a sort of autopilot; my emotions were numbed and I felt detached from what was going on around me. "Just fucking move." I had no idea what I was doing. I had no plan, apart from continuous movement. The only thought in my mind was that I should act like the heroes I'd seen in movies, and take some sort of control over the situation. Yet despite my resolve, I felt like shitting myself.

Becky must have seen something in my eyes – the flickering flame of intent, perhaps – and knew that this was not the time to argue. She allowed me to push her away from the meeting room, shoving her ahead of me as we advanced towards the nearby fire stairs. Whatever few members of staff had been present when we arrived that morning were gone – the office was empty, the desks unmanned, the few active computers spilling green light.

Sirens wailed outside, and I heard the buzzing chop-chop sound of helicopter blades in the skies above the office block. Whatever had begun last night, ceasing just before dawn, was now back in full swing. People were killing themselves all over again, only this time they seemed more intent on finishing the job.

We descended the fire stairs and entered the main lobby, where the security desk was empty. An open copy of *The Sun* newspaper, thinner and with fewer pages than was usual, caught my eye: the headline read "Kamikaze Britain". I felt sick; I felt empty. I didn't know what I felt. Just dead inside.

"Where's Mitch? Where is he?" Becky had turned around and planted her heels; she was going nowhere until I gave her something that would help her to cope, even for just the few minutes it took for us to leave the building.

"He's not coming." I grabbed her by the arm and forcibly led her to the main doors. I knew she'd understand eventually, and that I meant no harm by my actions. I wanted to get us both to safety; that was all… if the concept of safety even existed in this insane new world.

Outside was chaos. People ran across the road, heading in random directions. A lot of them were screaming, some of them were yelling into mobile phones, and yet others were jabbing at handsets trying to get a connection. The networks would be going into overdrive, with everyone trying to contact their loved ones.

"This way." I moved ahead of Becky, still holding her arm. It was only when she saw Mitch's body, contorted into a human question mark among the other crumpled remains on the pavement, that I realised my error. Blood was still running into the gutter, a tiny trickle of red. Mitch's eyes were blank, shiny, and devoid of the warmth they'd held when he was alive. Turner's were black as onyx.

Becky fell instantly to her knees, her hands going up to grab her hair. She was screaming, but no sound came out of her mouth: her lips were wide, her white teeth flashed in the low sunlight, but she was unable to fully give voice to her horror.

I reached down and pulled her to her feet, using brute force to get her moving again. "He's gone… it happened so fast. Nothing I could do. All of them, gone." I was babbling, barely even aware of what I was saying, but the words seemed to galvanise Becky. I already knew that she was a strong-willed person, and her reaction was even more evidence of this. She set her jaw, looked away from her lover's body, and I pulled her in the direction I'd indicated.

It seemed as if everyone who had made it into the city that morning was now outside, in the streets. It was mayhem, people fleeing everywhere, sirens wailing, and emergency vehicles mounting the kerbs. There was no real purpose to any of this activity; it was all just kinetic energy. I saw people colliding with each other, slamming into walls and doors. Nobody had a clue where they were going or what they were doing. Blind panic ruled.

Just then I saw another army vehicle moving along the street. Foot soldiers marched ahead of it, this time with their guns held aloft. Someone had set a fire in the revolving doors of a solicitor's office, and charred paper and black plumes of smoke billowed out like dark phantoms.

We ran back towards St John's Wood, past the edge of the park.

There were more helicopters in the sky now and when I looked up I saw that some of them belonged to television news channels. It was an obscene sight: sky jockeys vying for the best shots, risking their own lives to get some footage that just might make their name. If they even survived this thing, whatever it was…

I could think of no other destination than the HumBird Inn. My mind focused on the place, like a Sat-Nav device catching a signal. We were running hard but I was still breathing easily. It felt like I could run all day.

"I don't believe this. I don't fucking believe it." Becky was repeating the same sentence, or crude variations of it, under her breath as she ran. Her hands were clenched into fists and her arms pumped. Somewhere she'd kicked off her work shoes and was sprinting bare-footed, like an Ethiopian marathon runner. We continued in silence – apart from Becky's mantra – and I hoped that once we were away from the well-worn city thoroughfares we could stop for a rest. My body was still keeping up the pace, but I was aware that this was a result of the massive amount of adrenalin now coursing through my system. Once that chemical reaction began to fade, we'd both start to suffer.

The sirens faded behind us, and (as we cut down unfamiliar side streets) so did the sound of people wailing and screaming and swearing. I didn't want to think about the other sounds: heavy thuds, like bodies making impact with the concrete pavements.

In what was a surreal moment, a burning car drove slowly past us. It was a red Ford Focus, and the fire had been started inside the car. Yellow flames licked out of the open windows, clutching at the roof and blistering the paintwork. A thin, blackened figure sat behind the wheel, still somehow managing to guide the flaming vehicle in a straight line. I saw his grinning white teeth, the crisped, still-blackening skin around his empty eye sockets, and then I looked away, unable to even process such a shocking image.

If Becky even noticed the car, she exhibited no reaction to the ghastly sight. She just kept on running, and staring straight ahead, as if hell were at her heels.

The hotel, when we reached it, proved to be less of a sanctuary than we'd hoped. We both stopped running at the same time, Becky stumbling and almost pitching forward onto the ground as she tried to halt her momentum. A huge National Express coach had ploughed into the side of the hotel, bringing down part of the main external wall and destroying the bar and dining area.

There was a dining chair sitting on the verge. A beer pump stood at the kerb. Several shelf units had somehow remained intact, and looked as if they were hanging in mid-air within a geometrical framework of dismantled brickwork.

"Oh, God…" Becky leant against a lamp post. She was sweating. Her upper lip trembled.

"We have to keep moving." It was easy enough to say, but I had no idea where to go or how to get there. It just seemed like the right idea: never stop moving.

The driver of the crashed bus was dangling half in and half out of the broken windscreen, surrounded by a silvered web of shattered glass. One of his arms was bent up his back at an odd angle and the other looked like it had been jinked out of its socket. The top of his scalp had been partially peeled away in the crash.

Some of the passengers had crawled from the wreckage alive, but thrown themselves onto the mat of broken glass and proceeded to slash at their own bodies. Blood and open mouths; makeshift daggers and clumsy wounds in the bared flesh. Those who had been unable to leave the bus had probably just died in their seats, but I could not bring myself to inspect the site any closer than was necessary.

Becky was throwing up against the concrete base of the lamppost. She'd brought up what she could and was now dry-heaving, her back bent, hands gripping the post so hard that her knuckles had turned white. Her eyes were bulging and one of her feet was turned inward, angled towards the other. She looked like a rag doll given rude life: a puppet that was not yet used to independent movement. I went to her and rubbed her back. She barely even noticed my touch.

After a few minutes she stopped heaving. A minute later she looked up, her eyes wet, vomit on her chin. She wiped away the mess from her face with the sleeve of her suit jacket, closed her eyes, and gritted her teeth. "What now?" She turned to me, and her eyes were rimmed with red. "What the fuck do we do now, Mr. Hero?"

I tried not to be hurt, but her words hit me hard. "What the hell was I supposed to do, just leave you there?"

She stood up straight, adjusting her clothing, and stared into my eyes. "What the fuck is there for me out here?"

"You have to know…" I felt like a shit for what I was about to say, but I needed to ground her fast; I *had* to bring her back to reality, whatever it took. "You might have loved Mitch, but he didn't love you. He would never have left his wife."

She slapped me hard across the face, her hand flicking out so fast that I only registered the movement after it had already happened. The pain barely even reached me.

"Don't you think I already know that, you shit? I always knew he was married." She walked away, limping slightly. Lactic acid build-up in her legs. She needed to stretch, to get the blood moving, but the spiteful side of me thought: *Fuck you, bitch.*

I turned away, glanced at the wrecked bus and what was left of its passengers, and then turned back to Becky. She was looking at me again, but this time her features were softer. The anger was spent. "I'm sorry," she said. "I know what you were trying to do. Thanks."

I nodded. She was rubbing her thighs. "Stretch them out. It's because of the running. You need to get the circulation going again, or you'll be aching even more in a few hours. And I reckon we have a lot of walking to do."

Becky bent over and touched her toes. She was pretty limber, and the sight of her cooling down like this after what had just happened bordered on the absurd. She looked like she'd been for a quick lunchtime jog… in her bare feet and her business suit.

I walked to her side and waited until she was finished. She took out a pack of cigarettes and offered me one. "No, I don't. Not any more." She shrugged and lit up, closing her eyes as she inhaled. She was a beautiful woman, even now, even in the middle of all this death and chaos, and I could see why Mitch had been drawn to her. Apart from her looks, there was a kind of intensity to Becky, a partially-glimpsed strength which suggested although she might bend a little she would never break. I wondered what her story was, what she had been through before this. Because we had all been through something before this… every damn one of us.

"What's your plan?" She had smoked the cigarette down to the filter. I watched as she stubbed it out against a lamppost we passed before throwing it away.

"I don't have one."

"I figured that." She looked along the road, in the direction we'd come from, and then back at me.

"I need to get home. To my wife."

Becky nodded. "Okay then. I'll come with you." She pushed away from the wall and turned in a slow circle. "So which way's north?" She smiled but it went nowhere near her eyes. I doubted that her eyes would ever smile again.

"Why would you do that? Don't you have someone here, in London? I mean, someone you care for?"

The smile was gone; in its place there was only emptiness. "The only person I ever gave a shit about looks like pizza on the footpath back there. All I have left is an uncle, in sheltered accommodation near Middlesbrough. I hate the senile fucking bastard, but it's the only destination I can think of. We might as well travel together than go it alone."

I wondered if her hard shell hid something more fragile, then realised that I hoped it didn't. If we were going to be travelling companions, I'd rather have a bitch at my side than a flighty, neurotic mess. It was not a nice thought to have, but I realised that nice thoughts were now a luxury, and one we could no longer afford.

"Come on, then. Let's get moving. I want to be well away from this place before it gets dark. We need to get some safe shelter if we're going to stay alive."

We walked north, the two of us, each heading towards our own vague goal. I took out my mobile phone and sent Kay a text message:

I'm safe. Call you at the usual time. xxx

I knew I could have taken a moment to call her, before we went too far, but by then I was already clinging to the routine, the ritual. It might be the only thing left to hold on to, and at some point further along the road it could even save my life. Things had changed, life was now about survival, and we all had our own lights to guide us through the darkness that lay ahead of us.

CHAPTER 9

St. John's Wood tube station was locked up tight, full-height metal gates pulled across the narrow entrance and secured by heavy-duty chains. It was a small station, and I'd only ever used it a couple of times, but it was on the Jubilee Line – which was one of the main routes from north London into the centre, cutting across from the north-east to the south-west of the city.

Becky and I crossed the road to join the small crowd of people waiting outside the station. None of them looked dangerous; they were all simply milling about as if waiting for something to happen. It felt like there should have been more of them there, and I wondered briefly how widespread these suicides had become.

"It's closed, mate." A man in a scruffy London Underground jacket and faded blue jeans wandered over towards us, holding his hands out at waist level, as if he were trying to calm a barking dog. "Sorry. Most of the system has been shut down for the time being. Nobody's told me why, so I can only assume it's because of this trouble. As if I bloody care." I could barely believe the old guy's blasé attitude. Was this a modern representation of the mythical Blitz Spirit, of which we heard so much in the southern media whenever some sort of tragedy struck the capital, or did he just not care very much?

I swallowed my northern cynicism and smiled as best I could. "Any news of when things might be running again? I have to get to King's Cross and catch a train."

"You and every fucker else, mate." The man laughed, shaking his head. "Give it a rest, eh? No trains are running – not from this city. Haven't you seen the news?" I heard the distant, muffled thud of what I thought might be an explosion. "The whole country's in a mess. Some kind of terrorism – chemical warfare, they reckon. Something in the water making people top 'emselves."

Becky shuffled at my side, tensing as if she were ready to either punch the man or run away at any moment: fight or flight. I glanced at her, raised my eyebrows, and then looked back at the station man. "Thanks for the info. I suppose I'll have to find another way north."

The man turned away and strolled back towards the gates, pushing through the cluster of bystanders to check the lock and chain he must have fixed there earlier – or perhaps it had been there when he arrived, and he was focusing on his duties to take his mind off a situation which was rapidly tilting towards the apocalyptic. I understood his attitude: sometimes if we pretend not to care the darkness recedes a little.

"So that's it, then?" Becky had lit up another cigarette. She was sucking back the smoke as if it was the only thing keeping her going. Perhaps it was.

"Could I bum one of those off you?" It was Bob, the manager of the HumBird Inn. I'd never known his surname, so addressed him by his Christian name whenever we spoke. I was sure I must have been told it at some point, but had failed to retain the information. I had clearly not considered it important then, but it might be now. The same could be said of a lot of things, I suddenly realised with a little jolt of shock.

"Hi, Bob. I'm sorry about the hotel... we saw the mess back there."

He shrugged his shoulders. "I'm the manager not the owner, so it means sod all to me apart from the fact that I'm out of work."

Becky handed him a cigarette, and he smiled at her. "You're Becky, aren't you? The name's Bob Willis. We've not properly met, although I've seen you with these two fellas before...hey, where *is* the other one? Mitch, isn't it?"

I looked at Becky, afraid that she might crack, but she managed to keep her emotions in check. "He... we lost him. This morning. When everything kicked off again."

Bob's face went red, a faint wine stain spreading out across his cheeks. "Oh. I'm sorry. I didn't mean anything by that." He lit his smoke and sucked on it, glad of the distraction.

"No worries. You didn't know." Becky smiled. It was slight, barely even there, but better than nothing.

"Listen," he said, changing the subject. "I heard you say that you're heading home, up north. I popped out to see if I could get some fags, but once we're done here I can take you as far as the Midlands if that's any good to you. My mother lives outside Birmingham. She's all I have since the wife left me. I figure that if I leave quickly, I might be able to move on the roads before they start to clog up with too much traffic." Bob was a big man – huge, really, standing well over six feet – but he had a kind face and a gentle demeanour. I thought that we could trust him, and he was certainly not displaying any kind of suicidal tendencies. "Well? Make your mind up. I'm leaving as soon as I finish smoking this." His gaze darted downwards to indicate the stubby cigarette he held in his hand.

"Thanks." Becky stepped forward, her bare feet shuffling across the concrete. "That would be great. Can I ask a favour? Do you think... well, would there be any shoes back at the hotel?" She looked down. Bob's gaze followed hers, and he smiled.

We followed Bob Willis back to the HumBird Inn. He barely even glanced at the ruined wall and the wrecked bus as he opened the side door and went inside. "Stay there," he said, looking back at us over his shoulder. "It might be dangerous. I'll get the car keys and some shoes for you." He smiled at Becky. It was a good smile, a nice smile. I could tell that it was making her feel better about things.

We waited in silence for several minutes. There was not much left to say, and Mitch's name was off limits while the wound of his passing remained fresh and untreated. Perhaps when we were a hundred miles or so along the motorway we could speak of him again, and perhaps even begin to share our grief. I hoped that we could find a way to mourn him together. He would have liked that.

"Here, catch these. I hope they fit." Bob appeared from the doorway, tossing a pair of battered white Nike running shoes at Becky. She caught one but the other dropped to the ground. She sat down on the retaining wall that surrounded the grass verge in front of the hotel to put them on.

Bob shook his car keys, making them rattle. "It's underground, I'm afraid, right along the far end. The inside access is blocked by fallen masonry, so we'll have to go down the ramp. It might be better if we all go down there together. Just in case..." I did not have to ask what he meant.

"Perfect fit. Well, as long as the laces are pulled tight." Becky slid off the wall and stood at my side. She placed one hand on my shoulder, and I understood on some level that the momentary contact was a display of trust. The ice around her seemed to be melting slowly; in a few hours we might even be real friends. I'd only ever known Becky through Mitch, and he had acted as a social filter. Now, with his absence sitting between us, there were layers of awkwardness we had to find our way through in order to connect. The dynamic of our relationship had altered fundamentally, and not only because of what was happening around us. Without Mitch, we were forced to get to know each other all over again – but properly this time, and without the safety net of his presence.

"I'll lead the way. Becky, you get in the middle, and Mack here can bring up the rear. I don't mean to sound too paranoid, but we have to be careful. It's dark down there. The lights are out, I checked. The power seems to be playing up. It won't be long before it dies altogether." I was impressed that he did not condescend to Becky and suggest she wait on the street while we men went down into the dark. Even Bob, it seemed, sensed her inner strength and classed her as an equal.

We formed an odd little procession as we made our way to the car park entrance. Standing at the top of the concrete ramp, a hand on the shoulder of the one in front, we must have been an almost comical sight. Then, before we could change our minds, Bob led us down the ramp and into the dusty dimness of the hotel's cramped underground car park.

The dark seemed to wrap around us like a mist, deepening as we descended into the belly of the low-ceilinged underground space. The smell of exhaust fumes was strong but not unbearable. There were no immediate sounds to be heard down here, or so it seemed, and those behind us – the peal of sirens, distant voices, the barking of dogs – receded as if someone were turning down the volume on a radio. Then, as we hit the level area at the base of the ramp, the subterranean noises at last became audible: the steady drip of water, rattling pipes, a strange high-pitched whirring noise that I could not identify, the soft rush of air being channelled through underground vents.

Standing there, and pausing for a moment to peer into the underground car park, it felt as if we'd entered another world. The upper regions were shut off, taken out of the equation, and all that remained was whatever we found beneath.

The first thing I made out in the gloom, as my eyes gradually became accustomed to the lack of natural light, was a woman dangling from a thick roof beam. She had fashioned a makeshift noose from a long, woollen scarf, looped it over the support beam, and then probably jumped off the bonnet of the nearest car to hang herself. We all saw her at the same time, and I heard Becky take a sharp, whistling breath. Bob shuffled his feet, as if planting them more firmly on the concrete, and coughed softly.

"Keep going," I said. "Becky. If you want to go back up, we'll understand. No shame in it."

She turned to face me, her cheeks drawn and pale in the darkness, clinging like paper to her cheekbones. "I've seen those films. The ones where the woman stays behind and gets killed. Fuck that. We stick together."

I nodded. Bob continued along the central aisle, his head locked into a forward position. It took me a few moments to realise why he was not looking to the sides, and when I did I hoped that Becky had not noticed what he was trying to ignore.

In many of the cars, sitting behind windows steamed and streaked with agonised last breaths, were people who looked more like life-sized dolls or dummies. Peering closer, yet trying not to draw Becky's attention to the terrible sight, I was shocked to see lengths of rubber hose trailing from the tops of a few windows that were notched open just a crack. The hoses were attached at the other end to the vehicle exhausts – God knows where they'd found the hose (perhaps it had been a fire hose they'd ripped off the wall), but somehow those crazy people had managed to divide a longer piece into these smaller lengths and patiently thread them through the gaps in the windows. The thought of the suicides being so organised was somehow even more horrible than the actual deaths. None of the cars near us was running; the fuel must have run out, the engines died. But up ahead, in the next row, I could hear the rumbling of still-active car exhausts.

"Shit," said Becky, signalling that she had now also seen what we had. "Ah, fucking shit on a stick."

"Keep looking straight ahead." My voice was wavering near the edge of hysteria.

"Don't look." Bob kept walking as he spoke. "Just walk."

The thought had not occurred to me before, but right now it scared the hell out of me. If we got down there, to Bob's vehicle, and were unable to get it back up and out onto the street, it meant another trip on foot through this particular circle of hell. That was something I had no intention of doing.

Just as the thought left my mind, I saw the Minivan. It was one of those new ones, the remodelled versions of the old classic Sixties design. The driver had rammed it into the rear wall of the car park, perhaps more than once. The windscreen was shattered. He was sprawled face-down across the bonnet, broken glass fanned out around his head like a reflective halo. He looked like some kind of abstract art installation.

"I can't believe this." Becky grabbed my hand; her grip was fierce. "Somebody tell me I'm having a nightmare."

No one answered, so she fell silent. Her feet dragged on the rough concrete surface, the soles of her newly-acquired trainers scuffing like those of a child being led reluctantly to school.

We passed the Mini van and shuffled onward. I was glad that this was not a deep car park. It felt like if we stayed down there too long we might never resurface, that the place would claim us as its own. I kept imagining that something was brushing my cheek – perhaps dust or cobwebs – but fought the urge to knock it away. There was nothing; it was just my imagination. The phantom sensation actually helped in some small way, because if I could imagine such a thing then surely the rest of this could also be down to my brain malfunctioning? That way I could pretend that none of it was real and deal with it later.

Such are the tiny hopes we cling to; hopes so easily dashed by the onset of reality.

We reached the end of the walkway. There were more mannequins sitting in cars down there, but there were also other figures sprawled on the floor, their hands clutching at the grey concrete, their mouths open. Some of them lay on their backs, eyes wide and staring at the ceiling. Their mouths were dark shafts into which had poured the essence of blackness: an absolute absence of light and life. It was impossible to tell if these people had been murdered or had in fact taken their own lives. I tried not to look at the patches and splashes of blood.

"It's over there. The dark blue Beamer." Bob increased his pace, veering towards an old BMW that looked like it had been parked there for years. A fine layer of dust coated the paintwork.

"Please tell me this thing will start."

"She might be a bit grubby, but she's never failed me yet." Bob unlocked the door and climbed inside. Becky and I stood to one side, out of the way. She leaned into me, clutching my arm. I was rigid, afraid to move in case she shifted her position and robbed me of this moment of intimacy. We watched Bob as he fumbled with his key ring and then, at last, he bent his head and slipped the key into the ignition.

The engine purred into life on the first try.

I almost let out a whooping yell, but the dense atmosphere and the presence of so many dead bodies stilled the sound in my throat. "Let's go," I said, gently shoving Becky ahead of me. "This place is history." There seemed something profound in my statement, but I could not quite grasp what it might be.

Becky climbed into the rear of the BMW so I took the passenger seat. The interior of the car was just as grubby as on the outside. Old parking tickets were piled up along the dashboard, a tattered tree-shaped air freshener, its scent long gone, hung from the rear-view mirror, and the foot wells were filled with crushed Starbucks coffee cups and crumpled Greggs' bags dusted with ancient pasty crumbs and daubed with grease spots.

"Nice. Could I have the number of your cleaner?" Becky's voice, from the back seat, took us both by surprise. Bob even managed a low chuckle.

Bob guided the car out of the parking spot, steering past the prone bodies as we made our way towards the ramp. We all stared straight ahead, through the dirty windscreen. The water jets came on, then the wipers. We lost our vision for a few seconds while the wipers simply smeared all the filth across the glass, but soon it cleared and we could see again. I'm sure we all took a silent breath as we passed the dangling form of the girl with the scarf.

At the bottom of the entrance ramp, positioned in the shadows so that we had missed him when we first came down, crouched the burned remains of a young man. His legs and lower torso were a blackened mess, but his upper body remained intact. He had died with such an expression of serenity on his face that I knew I would never be free of the image. His lips were curled into a contented smile, and his eyes were open. Open.

His eyes… they were *open*. And they were black.

"Oh, God. Oh, fucking hell." We were growing accustomed to Becky's expletives. I even found them oddly comforting: a dash of harsh reality in what felt like such an unreal situation.

Then we were back outside, and the horror of what we had found could be left below, where it belonged – because things seen below should never be brought up into the cold hard light of the surface world, where they can be viewed without a concealing blanket of darkness.

"Are we going now?" Becky leaned forward, with her head between the front headrests. "Can we leave?" She sounded like a child. I almost expected her to say *Are we there yet?*

Bob nodded in silence. He steered north, his lips locked together and his eyes never leaving the road. Whatever horrors we faced up ahead, before we reached the end of our journey, we all knew that we would never forget that underground car park and the dreadful sights it held. It seemed to represent more than we could put into words, so none of us ever mentioned it again.

CHAPTER 10

"I nearly had something there." Becky was leaning across me from her place on the back seat and fiddling with the car radio. "I'm sure I heard some words."

"We can swap seats if you like. I don't mind sitting in the back." I adjusted my position, fidgeting slightly. The seats were leather-bound, and not exactly comfortable. I was sure that I could feel a loose spring prodding my lower spine.

"No. That's okay. I'll not be a minute. If I can just get this fucking thing to work…"

Sudden static roared from the speakers, causing us all to tilt our heads to the side and wince, and as Becky spun the dial more slowly we began to make out what sounded like a human voice.

"What are they saying?" It was the first thing Bob had said since we had emerged from the car park.

"Welcome back to the land of the living," I said, glancing at him.

He winked. "Just a bit shaken, that's all. Nothing to get excited about. Twist the knob slower, Becky – you almost had it then. It sounded like a news report."

Gradually Becky managed to tune into a local station, and amid machine-gun bursts of static, we were able to follow the rather garbled broadcast via short snippets of information given by a manic male voice.

"…*initial government estimates are that between forty and fifty percent of the city's population is already dead… London's streets and homes are filling with corpses… remaining government officials are stating that the cabinet is fragmented… the prime minister is said to number among the dead… everyone's killing themselves… the outlying areas are also affected… it's spreading fast, oh God, it's spreading so fast…*"

That was all we heard, but it was enough to explain a lot of what we had already experienced – the surprisingly empty streets, the countless dead bodies, the closed doors and windows, the burning buildings on the skyline. Something was driving people to mass suicide, and even those in charge of the country were being affected – and nobody seemed to know why it was happening.

"Fucking hell." Becky slumped back into her seat. She lit a cigarette without asking Bob's permission, but cranked open the window to let out the fumes.

I thought about the radio reporter's last statement: *the outlying areas are also affected...*

That meant that whatever was happening was no longer restricted to the city. It was spreading. I had no idea how fast it would travel or even if my thoughts on the matter were correct – that something was moving out from the capital, spreading like an infection through the veins and capillaries of the country – but I feared for Kay.

I took my mobile phone out of my pocket and cradled it in my hand. I had a text message from Kay:

Been listening to the news. Call me when you can. Should I be worried?

Her message at least meant that this madness had not reached as far as our home, and she was unaware of any imminent danger. I replied to her message, trying to ensure that I came across as calm and in control. The last thing she needed right now was to be afraid; the last thing *I* needed to do was to scare her.

Stupidly, I was still clinging to our ritual – that I ring her only in the evening, before she went to bed. I blamed this on the fear that was still flooding my system, and the fact that I needed something normal, some kind of familiar routine, to help keep me from losing my mind. But was there also the possibility that, if I spoke to her then, in the car with the others, I might break down and colour their perception of me? Even then, in the midst of a situation of increasing terror, I needed to maintain the illusion that I knew exactly what I was doing, that I was at the helm of my emotions and guiding the good ship Mackenzie Booth through those treacherous, rock-filled waters...

Then, before I had the chance to change my mind, the moment was stolen away from me, and my attention was forced onto the road ahead.

"Shit, what's going on here?" Bob slowed the car, but did not stop.

The army blockade consisted of a couple of sawhorses and some red plastic traffic cones, but it had effectively blocked the road. Two men in uniform, rifles held at port arms, stood motionless in front of the blockade, staring at our approach. The sky behind them was darkening, as if from an oncoming storm, and the air around them seemed to shimmer – but I knew the latter was a product of my imagination. I also knew that if I wasn't careful I'd start seeing monsters lurking in the shadows…and that was not something I wanted to be faced with.

Bob halted the car a hundred feet from the blockade. There were no other vehicles in sight.

The soldiers did not move. They continued to stare. We stared back, caught in a stalemate situation, and only after several seconds did I notice their eyes. They were either black or dark red – at this distance, it was difficult to be sure. I recalled the events back at the office, when old man Turner had dragged Mitch through the window to his death. It hadn't really registered at the time, but his eyes had been the same: big and dark and weird-looking, as if a haemorrhage had occurred behind his eyes, in the brain.

Black blood. Dead blood. Blood on the brain.

The black-eyed soldiers kept staring at us, waiting for us to react.

"Look behind them," said Bob. "On the road, behind the road block."

He was right: there was something there. A body, lying in the road. I'd failed to notice it at first, because the army fatigues had blended with the scrubby foliage at the roadside, but a third soldier was lying there with the barrel of a handgun still wedged between his teeth. A spray of red flowers was tattooed across his cheeks.

"Why haven't they killed themselves? Isn't that the way this thing works?" Becky was getting ready to bolt; I could sense her panic filling the back of the car.

"I don't know…" I thought again of Turner, and how he had seemed to catch Mitch by accident, on his way to the window. But what if he had done it on purpose, if his intention all along had been to take someone with him when he ended his own life?

I was making all kinds of possibly crazy leaps of logic, trying to explain something that was completely inexplicable…but still, in the back of my mind, there was a slight itch of comprehension. Had I inadvertently stumbled upon the truth?

"Mow the fuckers down," I said through gritted teeth. "Do it now, before they kill us."

Bob did not need to be told twice. He floored the pedal and the car lurched forward, the rear wheels screeching on the road surface. We hit the blockade at a fair pace – fast enough, at least, to send the two soldiers flying into the air before they even had a chance to raise their guns. I wondered who they were planning to shoot, us or themselves. Or both.

The car took care of the flimsy road block, rolling over the plastic cones and knocking aside the sawhorses. I looked back as we drove away and saw that only one of the soldiers was moving. His friend was a crumpled heap in the middle of the road. The one still standing raised his rifle and stuck the end of the barrel between his teeth. He was still struggling to reach the trigger when I looked away. I wondered if his arms would be long enough.

Minutes later my question was answered when I heard the muted sound of a single gunshot.

TWO:
THE NEXT WAVE

He could not remember his family, his name, where he was, or where he had come from, but he could recall the moment when everything else had become clear. It was still playing out now, across the wide screen of his soul: a grubby little pub on a busy street, a tiny pain-that-was-not-quite pain at the base of his skull, a plate glass window, a running jump through the sharp-shattering pane...

The breaking glass had slashed and torn his face and arms, but there was little feeling. Just blood. Blood ran down his shirt, and stained his trousers, but he was barely even aware of it flowing. He had other things on his mind: an order, an imperative. As he ran, his thoughts converged to a single point. It grew in his head like a flower, taking up all the room and pushing out all other thoughts.

He needed to kill himself... he had to destroy this dead, already-decaying form, and join the rest of his brothers and sisters in that other place – a place whose location he could only begin to guess at, but which must be so wonderful. He knew it existed; this knowledge was what drove him. It was all he knew – along with the fact that he must crush, demolish, take apart the weak flesh-and-bone vehicle which carried him and had bound him to the rancid earth for so many wasted years.

It was as if someone had flicked a switch in his brain, and nothing else mattered but the primal urge for self-destruction.

He ran towards the woman with the pram. Others saw him, and moved the other way. Only the woman with the pram failed to notice him. She was looking at the baby, talking to it, perhaps even reassuring the infant that the world was safe and happy and held no horrors.

He hit her with all of his force, lifting her off her feet, and carried her with him... towards the edge of the motorway bridge. Cars and trucks and other things whose names he could remember but whose relevance remained a mystery travelled on the road below, making a noise like thunder. But even thunder was a concept he could no longer understand. He thought the word but it meant little to him now. He could just about hear the noise, but it came from somewhere below.

He leapt over the railings, carrying the woman with him. The pram was still back there, on the pavement, but he could not have everything. This one was enough, and others would follow. This he also knew: the knowledge coiled into life in the soup of his brain, shifting like a thin black serpent. It hissed. He opened his mouth in mid-fall and hissed too, joining in with a song that had been sung silently for eons: a song that could finally be heard.

He felt only exaltation as he hit the ground. The breaking apart of his body meant nothing to him; it was but a faint echo of feeling. He was completely unaware of his skull shattering like china, the bones of his arms and legs snapping, his ribcage compressing tightly around his chest to squeeze his silent, unbeating heart.

He did not die then, because he was already dead. He had ceased to be alive back in the grubby little pub on a busy street during a brief moment of pain-that-was-not-quite-pain. When everything had changed and he heard the song, that low, hissing chorus he had become so desperate to join.

No, he did not die; but his body was finally destroyed, freeing like a grub from its shell whatever flailing energy had been kept trapped and screaming within. Letting it out into the world, where it fled to the shadows, searching for others just like it. But what should have been freedom felt like yet another prison: there were no bars of bone this time, but still his essence was bound.

And when everything went black, he finally realised that he had been cheated. All his wretched life, he had been cheated, and he was being cheated still.

CHAPTER 11

We encountered the road bridge just as we left Bounds Green and turned onto the North Circular road. There were cars parked in a haphazard fashion beneath the concrete bridge, their doors open wide. A few engines were still running; the heat of exhaust fumes grizzled the air. Some of the vehicles – particularly the roofs – were spattered red, where blood from opened veins had rained down upon the bodywork. A single motorbike had been abandoned at the verge; its handlebars formed a strange design, almost like some representative symbol of what had occurred here, a cipher waiting to be solved.

At a guess, there must have been between fifteen and twenty of them hanging from the underside of the bridge. Their faces were bloated, some of them beginning to turn black. I stared at a woman whose shoes had fallen off, then shifted my gaze to a small boy – perhaps aged about six or seven – who dangled next to her, his bloodied legs limp and swaying gently in the breeze. They had used whatever they could find to hang themselves: coats, scarves, short lengths of rope and bungee from the boots of their cars. One man had even taken off his trousers, knotted them at the legs, and used the resulting garment as a perfectly serviceable noose. Before he'd jumped, he had slashed his left thigh, obviously going for the main artery as a back-up in case the trouser-trick failed.

So many of them had cut themselves before leaping from the bridge deck. So very many of them…

They all had their eyes open. Their black eyes. They were staring straight ahead, as if in the moment of death they had witnessed something that had scorched their vision.

Hanging, it seemed, was the most popular method of choice among those who were driven to extinction. I supposed it was a simple enough way to go: wrap something suitable around your neck and jump from a high place. If your leap was long enough, you might even break your neck and die instantly rather than slowly choking to death.

"How the hell are we supposed to get past this lot?" Becky's voice was strained, and when I turned around to look at her she was pressed into the seat, her eyes wide and fearful. "The road's blocked. We can't make it through."

I smiled, but it felt wrong, as if I were trying to cover up the mess with a cheap trick. "Don't worry. We've come this far, so I'm sure we can come up with something." I did not believe a word I was saying.

We stared at the view, each of us locked up with our own thoughts inside the close quarters of the car. It felt as if we each inhabited a small compartment within the larger space of the vehicle, and mine was becoming hotter and less comfortable with each passing moment. Like a cupboard wedged inside a tiny jail cell.

"I can drive some of those cars out of the way – the ones with the engines going. The rest we can push." I got out of the car, wishing that I did not have to move closer to the bridge. Standing with my feet planted on the central reservation, I stared at the bodies, at their black eyes, my gaze shifting to the side of the bridge above.

That was when I saw it: the graffiti. Drawn in thick red strokes the paint had dripped and smeared like blood (or perhaps it *was* blood; I could not be certain). The words, all three of them, were still legible.

THEY DID IT

I read them again, not understanding what the message meant. It seemed so random, yet at the same time there was surely a deeper meaning that I simply had not picked up during my initial perusal. I read those terrible words several times, and each time I felt that I was nearing some inscrutable truth of the human condition…

"They did what? Killed themselves? We can fucking see that." Bob was standing next to me. I had not even noticed him as he approached. He had his hands in his pockets, and had produced a woollen hat from somewhere to wear over his thinning, messy hair. "And *who* did it, whatever *it* is? That makes no sense. So why write it?"

"I don't know." I looked back at the painted words. "I don't know anything."

"Maybe… well, maybe they painted the words before they jumped. Like some kind of final message to the rest of us. Or a warning." He narrowed his eyes, as if he were beginning to understand his own tangled thoughts. Then, abruptly, he turned away. "Bullshit." He stalked back to the car, where Becky had now got out of the back to stand in the road.

There was no traffic in either direction, apart from the abandoned cars under the suicide bridge.

"Shall we get to work?" said Becky, rubbing her hands along her thighs. "It's getting cold." Her face was pale but her eyes shone; madness was trapped within them, behind the glaze.

"Be dark soon," said Bob. I looked towards the smudging sky and realised that he was right. Night came early at this time of year; the shadows gathered before you even noticed them. I did not want to be outside when night fell, moving the cars of dead people. I wanted to be somewhere safe, or at least somewhere that could be made safe. In that moment, even the cover of Bob's car seemed fragile and slightly pathetic.

We tried to keep our eyes lowered as we moved those cars still capable of motion. None of us wanted to look up, at the remains of people who, only a couple of days before then, would have been laughing, talking, loving, and enjoying their lives. It took us over an hour to clear a space wide enough to drive through, and during that time the sky took on several shades of darkness, swallowing the daylight as it approached late afternoon and an early evening.

The work was relentless, but it had to be done. There was no other way to get past. The task helped clear my mind of the horror, and I was almost reluctant to stop.

Near the end I found a bundle inside one of the cars, jammed into the rear foot well. Pale blue baby blankets, with something wrapped up inside. When I prodded the bundle, there was no movement – even when I prodded it hard, just to be sure. I had no intention of peeling back the layers of blanket to see what they concealed, but nor did I want to abandon an infant that was merely sleeping. A final squeeze told me all that I needed to know, when my fingers sunk in deeper than I thought they should have.

I drove the car into the bushes at the side of the road, turned off the engine, and walked away with tears in my eyes. I did not cry; if I let myself go, I might not be able to stop. I tried not to think of Kay's pregnancy, but it was impossible not to: our child was right there, inside her belly, and I would do anything I could to keep it safe. He-She. Our baby. Our future.

We were just about to get back into the car when I heard a voice. It was faint, distant, but someone was calling out.

Calling out to us.

"Hello!" The voice came closer, and I finally saw that a thin figure was moving towards us along the side of the road, making erratic progress. It was a young girl dressed in tight jeans and a long, overstretched sweater. She was almost running in her haste to reach us. "I'm okay – not one of them." I think we all knew what she meant.

"What shall we do?" Becky took an involuntary step backwards, towards the car. She raised one hand to her face, but did not touch it. "What if she's… you know."

Bob moved in front of Becky. "I think she's okay. None of them have spoken to us – remember those soldiers? They didn't even look capable of communication."

The girl was now only a hundred yards away. Her eyes were okay; big dark, but in a natural way. Not black.

She was young, pretty, a slight Asian female with blue streaks in her shoulder-length hair and a nose ring glinting in the dying light. "Hi." She stopped when there was something like fifty yards between us: a stretch of ground that could just as easily have been a hundred miles. She raised her hands. "I promise you, I'm fine. Look at my eyes. I'm not going to kill myself. Or try to kill you." Her eyes were indeed large and dark, but not the same kind of large and dark as the soldiers. Her skin was beautiful: that's what you noticed most about her. She was the most attractive girl I had ever seen.

"It's okay. What happened to you?" Becky had now stepped forward, accepting that the girl did not represent any immediate danger. She held out her hands as if she wanted a hug.

"My name's Manisa. I was coming back from a gig with friends and we hit some trouble. One of those suicidal bastards drove into us. They're all dead, my friends. All dead." Her face seemed to crack. I guessed that she had been keeping everything in, holding the emotions locked down tight until she could find someone to help her. Now that she had stumbled upon us, it all came tumbling out. "Dead…Fran, Dave, Tags…all *fucking dead.*"

Becky ran to the girl and folded her into her arms. Manisa wept loudly, and Becky responded hungrily to her need. The two women remained locked there, like a sculpture of mother and daughter, for longer than either Bob or I could stand.

"Where's your car?" Bob's scratchy voice broke into the moment, and the two women moved again, proving that they had not turned to stone. "Is it back there?"

Manisa smiled at Becky, wiped her eyes, and nodded. "Yeah. Back there somewhere." She waved her hand in the vague direction which we had been heading. "The road's a mess. There was a major collision: lots of vehicles involved. A fucking riot. Drivers were dragging people out of their cars and beating them, killing them. Killing them as they tried to kill themselves."

I cleared my throat. "How long ago was this, Manisa? When did it happen?"

"A couple of hours, maybe more. I've been sitting in a ditch at the side of the road, waiting for someone to come along. A few cars did, but the people driving them had those fucked-up black eyes. A couple of them crashed into the wreckage on purpose. They were laughing."

"Did you..." I had to ask the question. "Did you see what happened here, at the bridge?" I refused to look at the bodies.

"Yes." It was all she said; all that was required. I did not push her any further.

"We're heading north, to the Midlands and then up to the Yorkshire moors. You can come with us." Becky seemed keen to have another female along for the ride. Maybe she felt lonely, and I only served to remind her of what she had lost.

"My parents live in a suburb of Brum. The Midlands sounds great. I haven't been able to contact them – the phone networks are playing up."

I felt my trouser pocket, tracing the outline of my own phone. I hoped that I could get a signal later, when my scheduled call to Kay was due. As soon as I could get some time alone, away from the others, I would try.

"Glad to have you with us," said Bob. "Now, let's get moving. I don't want to be standing out here in the dark."

We all got back in the car. Manisa sat in the back with Becky; they were holding hands. It was good that Becky had found a friend. She needed someone right now – another damaged person to care for – and, even though I understood her compulsion, it made me feel envious that she had not yet reached out to me. My own feelings were confusing, barely formed, and instead of dwelling on them I tried to block them out. There would be time for self-analysis later, when we found some shelter from the oncoming night. I was trying so hard to be rational in my actions that my mental state was beginning to suffer. I knew that, and I also knew that I needed to address the situation.

Once we were moving again, it felt right to talk.

"Do you know much about what's happening?" Becky was still holding on to Manisa, as if the girl was some kind of link to the recent past, where everything was normal and Mitch was still alive.

Manisa's gorgeous eyes seemed to glow in the dimness at the back of the car. "We got caught up in a lot of shit last night, at the gig. We were in Cambridge, at a rock club. Somebody cut their own throat with a broken bottle, and then others started to do things – a man broke his own neck by diving head-first off a balcony, some kids set themselves on fire in the toilets: that kind of stuff."

"We know," said Becky, squeezing the other girl's hand. "We know."

Manisa took a deep breath before continuing. "Then, once we got out of there and back to our digs, everything seemed to calm down. The local news reports said that everything was under control, and things would be fine once the emergency services took over. They said it was some kind of mass hysteria, an outbreak of psychosis brought on by the stress of the fucking recession. They said it was an isolated event, localised. We knew they were lying, because we'd seen more stuff – even on our way back to the hostel where we were staying, we *saw stuff*."

The tyres hummed on the road surface. Bob dodged around stationary cars in the road, and bundles that looked like bodies but could just as easily have been piles of discarded clothing. We picked our way slowly through the wreckage. Manisa spoke faster, as if she were trying to ignore the evidence of the hell she was describing.

"This morning we decided to get back to London. The news seemed positive – they said it was all over with, that no one had killed themselves for hours. Then…" She swallowed hard, trying not to crack again. "Then we were involved in the crash. The craziness. By the time I was able to escape I was the only one left alive in our car. I stayed in there with the others in case someone saw me. I got out. I walked along the road and saw all those people hanging themselves and each other from under the bridge. There was nothing I could do, so I hid and watched."

The tyres hummed louder as we gained speed, leaving the wreckage behind. The sky darkened outside the car windows.

"They were helping each other, tying nooses, cutting open veins. Even little kids were joining in. I watched it all from the side of the road, hiding in a drainage channel. I watched it all…" She began to weep, but this time silently. "I *watched*." Her entire body hitched and she buried her face in Becky's shoulder. Becky stroked her hair. She was crying, too: crying for Mitch, at last.

We all cried for someone; but some of us did not want to show our tears. Some of us could not afford to let out our grief in case it drowned us.

CHAPTER 12

We made good time on the quiet roads. The basic plan – such as it was – had been arrived at without much fuss. We would head towards Solihull, where Bob's mother was a resident at an old folks' home in the area to the west of the town, and then carry on towards a place called Bourneville and check if Manisa's parents were still alive. After that, we'd all stick together and continue the journey up-country, towards West Yorkshire, and sit things out for a while at my place near the moors. The house was purpose-built for such a siege; it was a solid, old-fashioned construction, and the cellar was impregnable if it came to that...but I did not want to think about the cellar. Not just yet.

We talked in general terms, and masked our emotional connection to each separate stage of the planned journey. Bob spoke of his mother only in the third person – it was strange to hear him speak of "Bob's mother" – and Manisa did her best to describe her parents as "Mr and Mrs Sahib". It was a crude method of dissociation, but it seemed to do the trick.

For my own part, I did not mention my wife's name. I simply spoke of our isolated house, and what a good fortress it might make if we put in the work to shore it up against potential attack. I knew that she was safe, and had to believe the situation would not change in the time it took me to reach her.

And there was always the cellar...

It seemed almost surreal to me how few cars we passed on the road, and whenever a vehicle did come into view no eye contact was made between survivors. It was as if there existed a sheet of glass between individuals – or groups – and to even acknowledge these other desperate souls would mean that we would also be forced to fully acknowledge the catastrophic nature of what was happening to humanity. In a manner that I thought of at the time as typically English, we chose to make this a quiet apocalypse. It was not a case of the notorious 'stiff-upper-lip', but we did seem to be acting like characters from a polite, restrained fiction.

There were, of course, the constant reminders of the situation outside the car: bodies lying in the road or on the verge, abandoned vehicles with figures slumped behind the wheel or in the passenger seat, the remains of soft red detonations on the tarmac. The empty husks of many wasted lives.

As we passed level with Luton, the now inoperative airport located somewhere off to our right, we saw a group of men, women and children throwing themselves and each other off the roof of a tower block in the distance. A series of small black silhouettes locked in dance-like motion; brief sketches of people plummeting to their messy deaths.

"Leftovers" Manisa's voice broke the silence.

"What's that?" I looked in the rear-view mirror. The two women were just another couple of dark shapes.

"It's what everyone's calling them. I heard it on the radio while I was hiding in the car, after the crash. Some Deejay was still manning his station. He'd locked himself inside with food and water and was giving this stream-of-conscious report, more like fucked-up poetry than speech. He said that the best estimate was between fifty and sixty percent of the population had killed themselves, and the rest were divided into two groups."

Bob made a sound in his throat. It was almost a growl. I did not know what it meant.

Manisa continued: "He said, this bloke, that the rest of us were split into survivors and leftovers. The leftovers are still suicidal, but they want to wipe out as many of the survivors they can when they die. Like kamikaze squads, he said. They're taking as many people they can with them when they check out…"

The lights along the side of the road chose that exact moment to flicker and fail, and darkness made a fist around the car. Bob took his foot off the accelerator, and switched his lights from half-beam to high-beam.

"Leftovers," said Becky, from the back seat. She repeated the word another few times before pausing for breath.

"That's what he said. The Deejay. That's what people are calling them." Manisa sounded on the verge of tears.

"Well, it fits." Bob kept his eyes forward as he spoke. "I mean, isn't that what they are? Human leftovers? Did he say anything else of interest, this bloke on the radio?"

Manisa stirred, her clothes rustling. "He said that it isn't terrorism, and that nobody actually knows what caused it. They have black eyes and they lose their... their basic humanity. All they want is to smash their bodies into as many pieces they can. And they want to take the rest of us with them. A lot of what he was saying sounded crazy, but some of it... some of it didn't."

Becky shivered, leaned forward. I had thought she was sleeping, but she had merely been listening. "So what began as some kind of mass suicide bug has now mutated into something else... something worse. Is that what we're saying here? These things — these leftovers — are not only suicidal, but murderous."

Nobody answered her question, but I didn't think she was expecting an answer. She sank back into the darkness at the rear of the car. Manisa fell silent, too, as if the gravity of the situation had taken away her voice and stuffed her throat with darkness. Nobody really needed to say it out loud, but if the estimates we'd heard were correct that didn't leave a lot of survivors.

Up ahead there was another blockage in the road. This time a motorway flyover had been severely damaged. A helicopter sat buckled and broken amid the steel and concrete debris. I could see the pilot — or what was left of him — slumped half in and half out of the vehicle, and there seemed to be other body parts around him. I imagined that he had taken a dive into the bridge, spotting a group of people standing on the flyover below him. Perhaps they'd taken the high ground to look for help, and had even been waving, signalling to him that they were in need of aid.

The pilot had simply turned the helicopter towards them and let it drop. From the look of it, not one person had survived.

"I know another route off that last slip road we passed. The quiet way, along back roads." Bob turned the car around and we headed off the motorway until we reached a main road and then a single-lane turn off. The narrow road was surrounded by open countryside, and in the distance I could make out a dark line of trees like a row of soldiers. Towards the west, a single concrete tower block loomed above the horizon. There were no lights visible from its small, square windows. If anyone was home, they either had no power or were simply hiding in the dark.

We drove in silence for a while, the black outline of the tower block growing closer. The road veered away from the place at a distance of a few miles, and I think we were all glad that we did not have to pass any closer to its dark, silent and brooding bulk.

"I need a piss," said Bob, slowing the car. "I can't see anyone, so I'm assuming it's safe to stop for a couple of minutes." He pulled over into a passing point and stared through the windscreen. "You know, the longer we're in here the harder it is to get out." He glanced at me, smiled. I appreciated the gesture, but there was a stark quality to the smile that I found deeply unnerving.

"I wouldn't mind getting out, too." It was Manisa. She pushed herself forward, beautiful eyes wide and fearful. "If that's okay."

Bob nodded. "Of course it is. Those who need to go, go now. The rest of you, just keep a look-out. There could be anybody out there in the dark, but we have a clear view across the fields so should see them coming."

We all knew what he meant when he said 'them'. The leftovers.

"Okay." He opened the driver's door. "Let's get out and get this over and done with."

It was cold outside; I could see our breath dancing in the air. The body-heat inside the car had been misleading.

"Fucking hell," said Becky, rubbing her upper arms. "When we get somewhere, how about trying to find some warmer clothes?" She took out her cigarettes.

"Good idea," said Bob. "Right. Manisa and I will head for those bushes over there. I'll go one side, you go the other." He stared at Manisa, and she nodded, lips tight, hair falling across her lovely face. "I promise not to peep." She smiled, but it was guarded.

He turned to Becky. "I could use one of those."

Becky nodded and handed him a cigarette from the dented pack.

I watched as they climbed over the fence that bounded the road and trotted a few yards across the field. Manisa vanished into the bushes, and Bob went round to the opposite side. I glanced away, watching the fields at the side of the bushes. Nothing moved. I turned around, examining the landscape behind me. Again, the darkness was undisturbed.

"You sure you don't need to go?" Becky was staring at me, hugging herself and leaning against the side of the car. She had lit up a cigarette; its tip glowed from between her fingers. It was shaking. I wondered what she'd do when she ran out.

"I might just pop over there and try," I said, indicating the fence behind us, where yet more bushes formed a low screen. "Is that okay? I'm only a few yards away, so if anything happens…if anyone comes…"

"Go," she said. "I'm fine. Just come running if I start to scream."

I turned away and headed for the fence, taking the mobile phone from my pocket. I climbed backwards over the fence, so that I could keep the car and Becky, along with the bushes beyond, in my sight. Nothing moved. Nothing stirred. Not even the wind. Not even the birds or the wildlife in the undergrowth. It was eerie; as if every living thing was lying still, too afraid to move. Apart from us, that is: we were the only moving things in the landscape. Stupid, stupid us.

I did not need to urinate. What I needed was to speak to my wife, but I felt unable to express myself freely in front of the others. I lifted the phone to my closed eyes, praying that I could get a signal – Bob had tried to call the home where his mother was living earlier, and been unable to get through. Manisa had managed to send a text message to her parents, but had received no reply.

I opened my eyes. There was a single bar on the screen, indicating that it was picking up a small amount of signal. The other bars, the ones indicating the battery life, flickered between one and two, falling to one even as I watched.

"Shit." The power was failing all around us, and I did not have an in-car charger, so I needed to make this call count. I backed away from the bush, watching the glowing bars on the screen. The signal jittered, the bars rising. I felt the ground rising slightly beneath me, and as I walked backwards up a slight mound the bars reacted.

I now had three bars; enough of a signal to make a call.

Terrified to move even an inch, in case I lost the frail signal, I thumbed the phone and dialled Kay's number.

CHAPTER 13

— *Hello, baby. Are you safe?*

— *Oh, thank God. Thank God it's you.*

— *Are you? Are you safe? Tell me.*

— *Yes. Yes, I'm fine. I've been hearing on the radio about everything that's happening, but the radio went off a couple of hours ago. I managed to put some batteries in, but all I can get is static. Dead air.*

— *A lot of people are dead. The TV and radio stations will be empty.*

— *I know. Are you safe? Where are you?*

— *We're heading for the Midlands. I should be with you before morning. We just have to pick up a few people – if they're still alive – and then we'll all come for you. Have you locked up the house?*

— *Oh, you'd be proud of me, my love. It's amazing what a blind girl can do when she's backed into a corner…*

— *You always amaze me.*

— *I managed to close all the shutters on the windows and barricade the doors. It took me ages, and I had to keep resting because He-She didn't like me running around, but I got there in the end.*

— *You are okay aren't you? You'd tell me if you weren't?*

— *Yes. I'm fine.*

— *And He-She?*

— *He-She has been doing a lot of kicking, but He-She is fine. We can't wait to see you.*

— *I'll be there by morning: daylight at the latest. We've a strong group; we can put up a fight if we stay together. Those things...*

— *The leftovers? That's what they're calling them, isn't it?*

— *Yes, the leftovers. They're killing people. Like fucking kamikazes.*

— *Don't swear. You know I don't like it... not in front of He-She.*

— *Sorry. Like kamikazes. They're roaming around killing as many survivors as they can find, and doing away with themselves at the same time.*

— *I know. It sounds bad out there. Promise me you're being careful. No heroics. No silly risks.*

— *I promise.*

— *Say it. Tell me what you promise.*

— *I promise, baby. No heroics. No silly risks. I'm in control.*

— *And?*

— *And...*

— *And?*

— *And I'll keep safe for you and He-She. I'll be there to protect you.*

— *Good. I believe you.*

— *Where are you now? Upstairs?*

— *No. I'm in the cellar. Lots of food and water. Nobody can get inside. Remember that when you get here: I'm down in the cellar. I've locked the door and barred it from the inside, so you'll have to make a lot of noise. Say my name...I'll hear you.*

— *I can barely hear you now.*

— *The signal's weak down here. The battery's low.*

— *I love you, Kay.*

— *I know you do. And we love you. We both do.*

— *Kay? Kay? I can't hear you…*

— *Say my name… I'll hear you.*

— *I love you both.*

— *Say my…*

CHAPTER 14

My cheeks were burning, despite the chill. I wiped my eyes and looked at the phone in my hand. The battery was almost flat. Kay's voice had barely been as loud as a whisper by the end of the call, and her words had cut off before we'd finished what we needed to say. I looked up at the sky, at the stars and the blackness squeezed tightly between them, and an unwanted image began to form in my mind: Kay's face, her eyes black and blood-filled… her belly hanging loose and bloated, like a sack of offal…

But, no. *No.* I could not go there: I *would* not go there, and imagine that terrible scene. I had to keep telling myself that she was safe, and that I could get to her before anything bad happened. The cellar of our old house was the safest place I could imagine – probably the most secure place on earth right now.

She was safe. She was miles from town, with no neighbours nearby, and located underground behind a thick wooden door.

Safe.

She was safe.

They were safe: my wife and my unborn child, Kay and He-She.

I climbed back over the fence, my eyes still streaming – but I could blame the cold night air for that; the biting temperature out here in the middle of nowhere. My travelling companions did not need to know about my pain – they had their own to deal with, and there would surely be more on the way.

At first I did not realise what was wrong with the scene before me. I could see the car, the wide open doors, and the uneven shape of the bushes in the background. Then, like the result of a time delay, it all clicked into place and I recognised the flaw in the picture.

Becky was no longer standing by the car.

I paused, feeling colder and slower and heavier than I had only seconds before. Even the tips of my fingers burred with an icy chill. I thought that it might freeze me into immobility, but then the blood started flowing again and I was able to move, or at least to think about moving.

"Becky?" I stepped cautiously forward, off the narrow verge and into the road. "Where are you?" I was aware of the utter banality of what I was saying – even of the stupidity of my murmured questions – but that did not stop me from repeating them: "Becky? Are you there?" Part of me hoped that nobody would respond, because if they did I had the feeling it would not be Becky's voice I heard calling back to me in the dark.

A sharp movement caught my eye, drawing my attention to the field where Bob and Manisa had gone to empty their bladders. Shadows moving across the grass, soft and flighty, like oversized moths. Clear signs of movement.

Somewhere deep inside the human shell there is a place that reacts instinctively when something is fundamentally wrong. In the second before an airplane engine fails, the heartbeat before a bomb goes off, the finger-snap prior to rapid gunfire on a sunny street. Something, somewhere, within us *knows* what is going to happen, and our very soul tightens like a knot.

I knew. I knew what was wrong. I just had to let my mind catch up with whatever my body was already preparing for.

As I moved along on the far side of the car, I saw where Becky was now standing, rigid with terror. She had crossed the fence, and was motionless in the field. Ahead of her were the bushes, and to the right of the dark cluster of dying leaves and branches Bob was crouched with his trousers still pulled half way down his legs. He was clutching his belt, just about retaining his modesty, but the three figures standing beside him could not give a damn about such minor issues as modesty.

The skinny female at the front of the small group was covered in blood. I knew immediately that the blood was hers, and had come from the open wounds on her bared torso. Deep cuts ran across her small chest, and her belly had been slashed so badly that what looked like clumps of viscera were protruding from the openings. She was barefoot, and wearing only a pair of ripped jeans. I doubted that she could even feel the cold.

The other two leftovers – both of them male – stood slightly behind the first. They were staring at Bob with their artificially dark eyes. The one to my left had only one arm – the left one. The other arm ended in a messy stump just below the elbow joint; gobbets of gore matted one side of his smart business suit. His face was a mass of fresh contusions, as if he had spent quite some time slamming his face into a wall or diving from a height onto a concrete path. Absurdly, he was still wearing his necktie.

The other man was more or less intact, but one of his blackened eyeballs was impacted into its swollen socket; the other eye was also black as jet. As I looked closer, I realised that his lips had been removed, and what I had first thought was clown's lipstick smeared around his mouth was actually blood.

Nobody moved. Becky, Bob, the three battered leftovers...they were all completely still. It was like a painting, or perhaps a frame clipped from a movie. Such an odd tableau, and terrifying in the extreme. I held my breath in case I shattered the moment.

Then, finally breaking the spell, the leader of the three opened her mouth and began to hiss. The sound was like nothing else I had ever heard, and a hiss was merely the closest approximation I could think of. It sounded more like the static between radio stations; pure white noise pouring forth from a human mouth. *Human...* could they even be called human anymore, these leftovers?

I had not been noticed. I carefully edged my way along the side of the car. It was unlocked, so I knew that I should be able to open the boot to get at what was kept inside. Slowly, I made my way to the back of the car, and by a fluke of positioning I found myself standing directly behind Becky, which meant that the three leftovers would be unable to see me. I took my chance and opened the boot, my motions surprisingly smooth and quick, and then started rummaging inside. In the storage space I found a crushed cardboard box containing rusty cans of lubricants and de-icer, a folded-up picnic blanket, a partially deflated football, and a tyre iron.

I grasped the tyre tool, feeling its strength and solidity pour through my flexing fingers. This was it. Now I was truly in control. And, after all, isn't everything always about control? That was the thing, I was beginning to realise, with these leftovers of humanity, these dead-to-the-world remnants of how things had once been. They were no longer in control of their own bodies. Rather than exercising free will, they were driven by an external imperative: the desire for absolute extinction.

I turned away from the car, leaving the boot gaping, and strode calmly (oh, so calmly) towards the fence line. Still I had not been noticed. The stand-off up ahead was so intense, so focused, that I was able to get very close before one of the things turned and looked at me. It was the barefooted leader, the female with the ripped torso, and under her mask of blood I was sure that I saw her smile. She opened her mouth and hissed again. Up close, the sound was even more disturbing than I had first imagined... and even less human. It sounded electronic, as if artificially created by a software programme. Utterly inhuman.

Becky turned towards me, finally able to move. She staggered backwards, and I noticed that she was holding a large rock in her hand. Clearly she had been caught in two minds – whether to throw the rock or run to safety. Her breath was a thin white streamer. It hung in the air like a ghost.

Manisa lay on the ground by the bushes, not far from the three men. Her mouth gaped, her brown eyes blinked like those of a beautiful damaged doll. There was blood on her face; just a smear, but enough to tell me that she had been attacked and possibly hurt. Her right eye was beginning to swell.

I did not break my stride. Lifting the tyre iron, I went straight for the leader, and was pleased to notice that Becky threw the rock at one of the others in what was a purely instinctive reaction – later, when I asked her, she could not even remember doing so.

The leader's skull cracked on impact. I felt the jarring shudder travel along my arm, biting into my shoulder. I hit her again, ignoring her grasping hands, and kept on hitting her until she went down on one knee – a misguided proposal in a world gone mad.

"Kill them!" Bob had finally managed to adjust his clothing and shot out from the cover of the bushes, rugby-tackling the third leftover around his waist just as he was bending to deal with Manisa. For her part, Manisa rolled away and tried to get to her feet, but in her panic she kept slipping on the grass.

I did not stop hitting the leader until she went still.

Bob and Becky were taking care of the other two, using rocks and sticks they must have picked up while I was otherwise occupied. The fallen leftovers were silent; they did not even scream. They just lay on the ground, their black eyes open wide and staring, and absorbed the blows, accepting their bloody and brutal end. I could have sworn that they were grinning.

I walked over to Becky and grabbed her arm. Bob had already

stopped, and was doubled up dry-heaving. Becky's face was white with madness; her eyes had lost their colour, becoming stones set deep within the mask of her skull. She blinked a few times, and then seemed at last to recognise me.

"Nice work," I said, lowering her arm until she could take over the action herself. "You did well." My voice was low, but loud enough that she heard me.

Inside, I was a raging storm of pain and regret and bitterness. But on the outside, at the edges that I showed the world, I was cool and in control of the situation. My hands were steady, my skin was dry, and I seemed to have a purpose. None of this was true, of course; it was all just a sham, an act. I had always been good at hiding my true self from those around me.

It was all about *control*. That was all that mattered, and now it mattered even more.

I felt like weeping, but I could now allow myself to break. Those people were not people, they were leftovers. Whatever might have once been human about them was now long gone. If I kept telling myself that, repeating it like a penitent's prayer, I might even start to believe it.

"Thanks, man." Bob was now on his feet. He wiped his mouth with the back of his hand. Stringy vomit clung to his fingers like a sticky web. "We all froze. If you hadn't come back and seen us…I dunno. Thanks."

I put a hand on his shoulder but he shrugged it off, embarrassed. "It's okay, Bob. You recovered. You stepped in and did your part. Don't worry. None of us are the people we thought we were – this thing, this madness, it's making us realise exactly what we're capable of."

"And we're capable of killing. Of murder." Becky was crying, but silently. Tears streamed down her face, but her jaw was set. "We killed those people."

"No." I faced her, wanting her to hear this, to take it all in and assimilate the facts. "We killed those *things*. They weren't people, not any more. *We're* people – we're alive and trying to survive. They're not us, not now. They're something else. I don't know *what* they are, but it isn't human."

"Not human," she said, staring at the steaming bodies. "Not. Human." She had stopped crying; her barriers came back up before my eyes. "Not fucking human."

"Not like us." Manisa stood behind me. I turned. She smiled. "Thank you, Mack." She had wiped the blood off her cheek but I could see a small cut at the side of her eye, and the wound was leaking. "We all have to learn. To kill. To stay alive. Everything's different now, the world isn't the same. The rules have changed."

We all stood there, in the field, in the growing night, staring at each other. The faces we each saw had changed, too, over the last few minutes. They were hard and cold, like blocks of stone.

Suddenly we heard a strange buzzing sound, like swarms of bees approaching. Then there was tinny music, and I realised that what we were listening to was the sound of mobile phone ring tones. My own phone was vibrating in my pocket when I touched it with my fingers. I reached inside the pocket and took out the phone. The screen was glowing, pulsing.

Becky was holding her phone. Manisa was extracting hers from her jeans pocket. Bob did not have a phone, but he was looking over at the bodies of the leftovers – the same sound was coming from their direction; one of them must have had a mobile phone on him.

"Should we answer them?" Manisa was staring at me, and not at her phone. I glanced down at the screen of my own device. There was no message telling me who was calling. The screen was blank, but still it pulsed with a regular rhythm.

Then, at exactly the same time, all the phones stopped ringing.

"Fuck," said Becky. "I have a text message." She was holding her phone handset away from her body, as if she were afraid of it.

I looked at my phone. I had a text message, too, but again there was no indication of who it was from. I thumbed the buttons and watched as the screen flared, opening the text.

"Oh, shit. Shit Mack." Becky took a step back, away from me. "I don't want to know. And why are they ringing anyway?"

The message appeared on the screen. It was almost absurd in its simplicity, and I remembered the words daubed on the motorway bridge above the hanging bodies.

THEY DID IT
"Open them," I said, still staring at my phone. "Open them now."

Manisa did as I requested, but Becky was slower to react. "I...I can't, Mack. I can't."

I snatched her phone and pressed the button to open the text. The same words appeared on the screen, mocking me with their repetition. I looked up, at Manisa. She was holding out her phone, the screen turned towards me. I barely had to look at it to know what the message said. But I looked anyway. How could I not?

The message was deleted as I watched, without Manisa even touching the buttons. I checked mine and Becky's handsets and the same thing had happened. The messages were gone. Even when I accessed my phone's call log, there was no record of anything.

"We should go." I walked back towards the car, putting my phone back in my pocket.

"Who sent them?" Becky's voice tailed me, unwilling to leave me alone. "What the fuck is going on?"

I said nothing. I knew nothing. All I wanted was to get moving. The rest of it could wait until I got where I needed to be, and I could convince myself all over again that I was in control. Because right then, after those phone messages, control no longer felt within my grasp. I could not even lie and pretend that it was.

CHAPTER 15

We had an easy ride for the next part of our journey. I sat staring ahead, at the lonesome roads that wound their way through the open countryside, and Bob spoke softly at my side. The women were silent, too, for the most part. I heard the occasional snatch of murmured conversation, but little else filtered through to the front of the vehicle. We had entered some kind of lull, but I was convinced that the little group we'd formed would only take strength from such quiet moments.

The nursing home where Bob's mother had lived for the past five years was an old country house with its own grounds – it used to be a boarding school, but when that went bankrupt in 1994, during the last recession, things changed and it became what is quaintly called a rest home. Bob sent all his spare money there, to pay for her keep. This was a side of him that surprised me in some ways, but in others it seemed to fit what little I knew of the man. He was a cool, solid presence in our accidental troop, and I was glad that he had joined us.

Mrs. Willis was seventy-five years old, and Bob loved her in a way that should have been embarrassing in a man his age but somehow wasn't. He had never totally abandoned her, but nor had he been one of those men who lived with their mother way past the time when they should be moving out. No, Bob did not fit with any comfortable cliché; he was his own man, and he was proud of the way he had managed his life. He had gone through many lovers, even married once, but none of these women even came close to equalling or replicating the presence of his mother in his life.

"My father died when I was very young – four years old." His voice was a comforting hum in the darkness of the car. "Mum raised me after that, sacrificing her own happiness to make sure I grew up without a chip on my shoulder. There were no 'uncles', no strange men coming to the house to ruffle my hair and buy me presents while they wooed her. Mum just forgot about ever having another relationship and focused all her energy on making me feel like I wasn't missing out on anything because I didn't have a father in my life."

I stared ahead, listening to his story. It was a good story, which told of a tough woman making hard decisions in a world that was suddenly hostile to someone in her position. I knew all about tough decisions, and hostility had now become a way of life.

"She put me through University, and when a job came up in London she sent me packing. She didn't even cry when I left, but later she told me that she'd wept for several days. How could I not look after a woman like that? When she became ill, I made sure that I got her the best care I could afford. The dementia hit her hard. The last few times I visited, she didn't even know who I was. It hurts most when she mistakes me for my father."

I risked a glance at Bob, and saw the tears shimmering in his eyes. He blinked rapidly, trying to erase the evidence of his grief, but I had seen enough. I squeezed his arm, quickly and firmly, but said nothing. No words were required; the gesture was enough. Men like Bob do not give up their emotions easily, and when support is given it is required to be brief and unsentimental yet sincere. Bob was what some people call a rock, and he expected hard edges in return.

I glanced outside. Dark shapes that were lightless houses retreated surreptitiously from the edge of the road. We had seen no one for over an hour. The abandoned vehicles along this route were limited to a few empty cars parked at the side of the road. The occasional tractor stood stalled in a field. We saw no bodies, but we had already seen enough to taint our perception of the world – or what remained of it – forever.

We were running along roads parallel to the M1 motorway, and judging by the signs we passed I could estimate that we were several miles north-west of Northampton (although, God alone knew where we were exactly). We cut across country, going beneath the motorway on a grubby access road, and joined another B road, this one headed for the town of Warwick. What few communities we passed through lay in darkness, and we did not stop to see if there were any survivors hiding out in the lonely-looking buildings or staring at us from behind black windows. We kept on going, along sad little high streets, past deserted libraries and post offices and general stores, and then back out the other side of these hollowed-out places and into the bleak and endless countryside. Never looking back, just keeping our eyes locked forward, looking for the way that might finally lead us to safety.

At an out-of-town HumSave supermarket on the outskirts of Leamington Spa, we saw a large number of figures gathered in the car park. Bob slowed down, killing the lights, and we coasted by in darkness, hoping that we did not catch their attention.

"Who are they?" Manisa's voice trembled, filled with an emotion I did not want to understand. "What are they doing there?"

About half a mile farther on Bob stopped the car behind a petrol station and we got out, stretching our legs. "Want to take a look?" I don't know why I asked the question, and I doubt that Bob was completely sure of the nature of his answer; but he nodded, and we eased away from the car.

"Don't be long." Becky was smoking again. I wondered when she would run out. "How about popping inside there first? We could use some bottled water... and other stuff." There was no one around; the place was deserted, just waiting to be looted.

"Come on. Let's make this quick." I led the way across the forecourt, towards the single-storey structure which housed a small shop for essential on-the-road purchases like snacks and newspapers, a toilet block and a one-room office. The door was locked, but there was an open window around the side, near the car vacuum and air pump stations.

"I'm the smallest," said Becky, stubbing out her cigarette against the brickwork. She climbed in through the window as if it was second nature, and we waited for her to open the door. She vanished into the depths of the shop for a moment or two, and just as I was beginning to worry she reappeared with a large bunch of keys. Grinning at us through the glass, she tried several of the keys before selecting the right one.

The door swung open. "Welcome to Aladdin's cave," she said, stepping back to let us inside. Manisa stayed at the door, keeping an eye out in case we were joined by any unwelcome company, and the rest of us filled a few carrier bags with supplies – mostly bottled water, pre-packed sandwiches and chocolate bars for energy. Becky, I noted, ensured that she hit the cigarette shelf first. I kept an eye on the two short aisles and the open door to the office, just in case we had missed the presence of someone else in the store, but we remained undisturbed as we looted the shelves for provisions.

Back outside, I closed the door but did not lock it. Becky threw the keys into a planter by the empty newspaper stand.

"You take these back to the car. Bob and I will be back in less than fifteen minutes. Time us if you want."

"Take care," said Manisa, grabbing my bags. "Don't do anything silly." I was reminded of Kay's advice during our last, truncated phone conversation, and experienced a sense of longing that almost brought me to my knees. The feeling passed, but it did not leave me altogether.

Bob and I kept low as we moved in the opposite direction across the forecourt, past the pumps and the air hose, to halt for a moment beside the car wash. "You sure about this? I'd say it's the definition of the word stupid." Bob spoke softly, glancing around us at the darkness.

I nodded. "Yes, but they might be survivors. I'd feel better if we at least checked it out."

"I don't think so. I really don't think so." He looked at me, his eyes wide and intense. "I think they're… the *others*."

"I know, but just one quick look, to see what they're doing? Maybe if we understand what they're up to, we can have an edge. You know, give ourselves a leg-up next time we have to fight them off." It was the control thing. I knew it, but would never have admitted the fact. Knowledge is power and there is always power in control.

Bob nodded, but he did not look convinced. For my own part, I failed to completely understand my own motivation. It would be safer to return to the car and get on our way, but something was drawing me to the crowd across the way – perhaps it was simple curiosity, but now, in hindsight, it seems like something much more perverse, as if I were testing myself in the face of probable danger.

We crossed the road, walked for a short while along the verge, and then started to climb a short grassy hillock. The grass was damp underfoot, with frost forming on its surface, so we had to be careful not to lose our footing and draw attention to ourselves. We clung to each other like frightened children, but eventually managed to make it to the top of the rise. We stood behind the legs of a huge signpost advertising the shopping centre. It gave us a fine view – too good, if I'm honest. Some things are better when viewed from an uncertain vantage point.

It became immediately obvious that the people in the car park were indeed leftovers. There was no doubt in my mind of this – and I admitted to myself that there never had been.

It was bright down there; someone had lit a fire in one of the outbuildings and we could see clearly by its dying, guttering flames. In time, I came to wish that it had been more difficult to see.

Most of the leftovers bore wounds pretty similar to those we'd seen before, on the three who had attacked Manisa; evidence of self-mutilation impossible to ignore. Cuts and gashes and abrasions, bruises and scratches and even shattered bones. But some of them had gone even further in their efforts to self-harm, and we were appalled to see several of them with their cheeks or noses missing, ears cut off, and even one or two who had been scalped like victims in a Hollywood western. As we watched, many of them continued to defile their bodies. They used long knives, pieces of razor wire, even flames from makeshift torches which they grabbed from the last of the fire. Anything they could find was used as an instrument of self-harm.

It was a hideous spectacle, but I was unable to look away. There was something frighteningly compelling – and if I'm honest, weirdly seductive – about the sight of so many black-eyed figures calmly carving chunks out of their bodies, or setting fire to patches of their flesh. They registered no pain, no evidence that they could even feel what they were doing to themselves.

None of them spoke, apart from the horrible low hissing sound they all made, yet they seemed to be communicating at some primitive level, like intelligent apes. I could barely believe what I saw, but they had five or six survivors trussed up in shopping trolleys, and were pushing them back and forth, as if toying with them. If they had been able to laugh, I'm sure the sound of their glee would have been horrifying.

This went on for a few more minutes, and then they all stopped playing the game, a deep hush descending over the car park. Apart from the sounds of struggle made by those poor people tethered in the trolleys.

One by one, the leftovers opened their mouths and began to hiss: it was like an eerie song, a dirge one might expect to hear in a nightmare. The sound rose in volume, its tone somehow different from before, the rhythm quickening, and as we watched they slowly closed in on the survivors in the shopping trolleys. The separate hissing voices became one; a call to arms, a signal to attack.

The survivors struggled gamely, but they were trapped. One of them was already dead: he lolled in the cage of the trolley like a broken doll, his head and limbs dangling limply over the sides.

"Should we help them?" Bob grabbed my arm. His fingers dug into my biceps.

"What the hell can we do against so many?" I glared at him,

annoyed that he was even trying to pretend that we had a choice in the matter. "We'd be killed, too. You know that." He did not release his grip, and I began to use the pain as a way of distancing myself from what was going on at the bottom of the hill. It was all I had, that pain, and I hoped that Bob would keep up the pressure.

The leftovers were now pushing the shopping trolleys over towards the far corner of the car park, near a side entrance. A huge timber advertising hoarding had been torn down to reveal a long drop onto a sharp rock-fall below – perhaps it had once been a narrow river or drainage ditch, but now it was dry and filled with large, jagged stones. The advertising board was for a well-known brand of cornflakes. I do not know why I remember such a banal thing, but it seems absurdly important in the way that inconsequential details often do.

The survivors were trying to scream now, but some of them had rags stuffed into their mouths and it made things difficult. One of them – a young girl in her teens – tried to throw herself from the trolley as it was pushed towards the opening. She succeeded only in tangling herself in her bonds.

The trolleys were carefully lined up along the edge, their front wheels almost hanging over into the gap... almost falling, but not quite. Not yet. The leftovers stood back as if admiring their handiwork and the pause in proceedings seemed to last a lot longer than it probably did. At the time I hoped that it would last even longer; a single moment spun out across eternity, never coming to an end. But all too soon the leftovers began to move.

I knew what was coming – we both did. Of course we did. We weren't idiots.

The leftovers charged forward, at the trolleys. There must have been around fifteen or twenty bloodied figures gathered in the car park, and every single one of them ran full-tilt towards the trolleys perched so precariously at the edge of the drop. The front rank hit the trolleys hard, everyone going over in an instant – trolleys and bodies, all. The rest of them just kept on going. It did not take long, but once again my sense of time became elastic. A second became a day; a day became a week became a minute...

The whole thing lasted a lifetime but was over in seconds.

Finally, I turned away. I turned away and I tried not to vomit. Even after the muted cries of the survivors died down, the leftovers had continued to throw themselves over the edge in complete silence. It was unnerving in a way I had not thought possible. My mind buckled under the weight of the event. So much wasted life, so many unfulfilled dreams.

I turned to Bob, who was leaning against the sign. His hands were covering his eyes, reminding me of someone in a silent film. They were shaking. I reached out and tried to pull away his fingers, but he gripped his face even tighter, unwilling to look even now that it was all over. I could see his skin turning white where his fingertips bit deeply into it. "Come on, mate. I'm sorry I made you come along. I'm sorry I made you see. I'm *sorry.*"

It took a while, but Bob finally lowered his hands, and when he did I saw clearly that he had changed. His features had somehow rearranged into something unrecognisable. It took me a few beats to realise that he had been transfigured by horror. The Bob I had come to know, and to respect, was no longer there, and in his place there stood a different being, a man who – like me – had seen far too much to ever be the same again.

I wondered if my own face had changed, and then realised that it had probably been changing all along, slowly erasing all signs of the man who had gone before and creating someone entirely new to take his place in the world.

So, two altered men, we stalked back down the hill, along the roadside, across the petrol station forecourt, and stood by the car.

"Becky's inside, getting some more ciggies." Manisa looked dazed and confused, as if she too was struggling to recognise us. "What did you see over there?" Her eyes were dull; she did not really want an answer, not to a question like that. She was simply speaking to fill the silence.

"Leftovers," I said. "A lot of them. But now they're gone. *Gone.*"

Manisa nodded slowly, satisfied for now.

I think she was grateful that I did not go into any further detail, but I knew that she would not understand the true nature of that gratitude until much later. There were countless miles to go before true comprehension would come to her, and right then I did not want to be the one to force it down her throat.

"Gone," echoed Bob, staring at the ground. "They're gone."

Becky returned with her hands full, but for reasons we could not define none of us was able to look her in the face. I refuelled the car and then we climbed back inside. As we pulled away from the place I hoped that I would never pass by this way again. I was starving but I couldn't bring myself to eat any of the food we'd looted.

CHAPTER 16

The Woodridge Rest Home was several miles from the nearest town and surrounded on three sides by several acres of undulating land. Bob had already told us that all his spare money went on funding his mother's stay there, but he said it without bitterness or even the slightest hint of regret. She was his mother; it was what had to be done. Again I was struck by the man's basic dignity, his innate ability to simply carry out tasks that he saw as being necessary without even a murmur of complaint. A sense of duty was important to him.

"I'm getting a bad feeling," said Manisa. She had not spoken much since we'd left the petrol station, and I had been concerned by her sudden unwillingness to communicate. I guessed that she was tied up with thoughts of her parents and whether or not they had managed to survive. Even if they were alive, there was no guarantee that we would find them – they could have gone somewhere else to hole up while the world went mad around them.

"We'll be okay," I said, turning my head to watch her as she sat crouched in the back. "We've done fine until now, haven't we? We're a good team. As long as we stay together we'll get through this. I know we will." She flashed me a tiny smile and once again I was struck by her uncommon beauty.

Bob drove with more confidence now that he was on familiar roads, but I noticed that his entire body had become tense. He was worried about his mother, that much was obvious, but he also seemed to be preparing himself for something else. "If there's something wrong here, we get the hell out. Agreed?"

"What do you mean?" I glanced at him, but tried not to put too much emphasis on the question.

"From what we've seen so far, things have changed a hell of a lot over a short period of time. The rules are different now... if there are any rules at all." He paused, as if to allow his phrasing to sink in. "Over half the population has gone... and the rest are *different*. I don't think we can afford the luxury of trusting anyone until they've proven that they mean us no harm. I mean, we aren't even armed."

It was a fair comment, and I nodded to concede the point. "I'm with you. Let's just play things by ear, and if we don't like it we run. How does that sound?"

"Agreed," said Becky. Manisa added nothing to the discussion. She just sat brooding in the shadows at the back of the car. For some reason which irritated me I could not get her out of my mind; her face refused to leave me alone, even when she was silent. The light brown skin, those delicate features, and even the blue tints in her silken hair... I was forced to tell myself that I had a wife, with a child on the way. I could not afford to act rashly, even in such an extreme situation. Extremity, I told myself, was not a valid excuse for idiocy.

Then, as if rendering our conversation invalid, something came into view behind us. "Shit," said Becky, craning her neck to see out of the rear window. "We have company." The road behind us was taken up by a white van. The vehicle was moving slowly, as if herding us like a sheep dog with its flock, and several men walked alongside it holding rifles and shotguns. The men were all dressed in white boiler suits – like low-rent Hazmat outfits – and on their feet they wore heavy boots. They looked for a moment like a childhood image of Nazi storm troopers, marching along a road in search of victims; I half expected bombs to drop from the sky and fires to erupt along the smudged horizon.

"Who are they?" Manisa's voice was tiny, childlike. The muscles in my stomach tightened.

"Well, they haven't shot at us so I'm assuming they don't want us dead. Not yet, anyway." Bob's focus shifted constantly between the windscreen and the rear-view mirror. I was staring at the side mirror, feeling increasingly afraid and hunted. That was the word I held carefully in my mind, as if it were too toxic to share: *hunted*.

Bob guided the car along the road, focusing much of his attention on the mirror whilst also keeping us clear of ruts and potholes. Then, suddenly, the tarmac ran out and we were travelling along what amounted to a dirt access track. Due to some kind of optical illusion, the imposing structure of the Woodridge Rest Home rose slowly into view on our right before dipping back down again, as if it sat on a hydraulic lift and was being raised and lowered for our benefit. The old building was set back from the road and sat in a slight dip in the landscape, with trees surrounding it on the rear and sides. The only way to approach the place was from the front, along the road upon which we were already driving, and in full view of the people inside. It was the perfect place to defend, if that was what you wanted. And I had the idea that whoever had taken control of the property wanted exactly that. To defend it from anyone who meant it harm.

"What do we do?" asked Manisa, shifting her position. I imagined her thighs brushing against the leather upholstery, her hands making fists as they gripped the seat on either side of her body. In an instant, I pictured those same fists grabbing a bed sheet as she straddled me, and her thighs gripping my torso...

"We keep going. There's no choice now. They want us to move forward, so that's what we'll do. They aren't leftovers – that's obvious." Bob's jaw was tensed so hard that I could see the muscles working like small machine parts as he spoke.

"I'm not sure I want to know *who* they are." My words hung in the air, unchallenged. They stayed there for a long time afterwards, unable to escape the confines of the car.

We approached a high gate with razor wire strung across it like vicious Christmas tinsel. The fence it was attached too was also high – enough that it would be difficult, if not impossible, to climb – and it too was topped with lethal-looking lengths of security wire. Odd wooden platforms were positioned on the outside of the fence; some of these held what looked like bundles of rags, or even primitive effigies.

Standing on walkways along the inside of the fence were a few more armed guards. These ones looked relaxed, as if they were comfortable with weaponry – some of them carried guns, others had cricket and baseball bats, knives and axes and other assorted garden tools. One man had a chainsaw. I wondered if the thing was purely for show, to intimidate visitors. It was certainly working on me.

Bob stopped the car but left the engine running. The gate was slowly opened, and he glanced at me. "What do you think?"

"I think we have no choice. Let's go."

Bob nodded, then put the car into gear and inched it forward, going through the gates and into the flat, open space beyond.

"Fuck," said Becky. "Oh, fuck."

The white van at our rear entered the compound behind us, driving around Bob's car and pulling up near the fence. Two men closed the gate. They were wearing the same white boiler suits as the men with the van. I had already guessed, of course, that this was the vanguard of some kind of hotchpotch paramilitary group. What I did not know was who was in charge, and if he was hostile.

"Get out of the car and stand where we can see you. Do it slowly, and don't make any sudden movements." The man was standing by the driver's side window, his rifle pointed at the side of Bob's head. For his part, Bob kept staring frontward, through the windscreen. He was sweating.

"Okay. Just keep calm. We're not going to be any trouble!" I shouted in the hope that he would hear me through the closed window, and when he ducked down and nodded I knew that the message had got through. The man took a single step back, away from the car, but it was enough to convince me that if they wanted us dead we already would be. The man lowered his rifle, reinforcing my gut feeling that he did not have killing uppermost in his mind.

"We're still alive and these blokes could shoot us down in a second, so my suggestion is that we just go along with what they want until we know what the fuck's going on here." I turned my head. Becky and Manisa nodded. "Bob?"

He closed his eyes, sighed deeply, and finally said "Yes."

I hoped that Bob wasn't going to be any trouble, but thought that if his mother was either absent or dead he might just go ballistic and take out as many of these boiler-suited fascists as he could. "Just stay calm, mate. We'll see what's what and go from there. Okay?"

"Yes," he said again, but this time through gritted teeth.

Slowly, calmly, and smiling all the time, I opened the passenger door and climbed out. I thrust my hands into the air, where everyone could see them. "Okay?" The shit-eating smile hurt my face, but I managed to keep it going.

The man who had spoken to us nodded. "That's good. Now the rest of them." He had a young face and wispy facial hair. I guessed his age at somewhere between twenty-one and twenty-five at the most. He was a kid, just a fucking kid with a toy gun. But in the wrong hands, even toys can be deadly.

The others followed my lead and got out of the car. Bob came last. He was not smiling.

"Where have you come from?" said Wispy. He stepped forward, once again raising his rifle. He didn't quite point it at us, but the threat was implicit in his actions. The other men stood easy, watching the scene unfold. There were no women, just men. That made me uneasy.

"London. It's crazy back there." I lowered my hands to shoulder level.

"It's crazy everywhere," said Wispy. "Come on. Get in front of me. Doctor Thwaite will want to see you."

I led the way; the others followed reluctantly, as if they really wanted to bolt. I hoped that they would keep it together, that they could overcome the flight impulse. At least until we had the lie of the land inside the grounds of the Woodridge Rest Home.

"I want to see my mother." Bob's voice was low, filled with barely-repressed rage. "She's a resident here, in the home."

Wispy waggled the rifle barrel, indicating that we should keep walking as we talked. "You'll have to ask Doctor Thwaite about that. He's in charge here. He might know something."

Bob went silent, but I could sense the violence boiling under his skin.

We walked towards the main building, dragging our heels. A few other men had now joined Wispy, and they chatted amiably amongst themselves. There was little tension, apart from what I could feel coming from Bob in thick waves. Our escorts were untroubled, as if this was just another part of their day, a duty like any other which required their attention.

A small gate was opened to allow us inside the main grounds. As soon as we were through, the gate closed behind us. Somebody laughed.

In the distance, at the far side of the home, I could see people toiling in a field: some kind of night workers. They were surrounded by a low wire fence, and each of them looked to be hoeing or digging a patch of ground. A vegetable garden, I thought, remembering what Bob had told us about the place – that the residents joined in and helped by growing herbs, or feeding the chickens if they felt up to it. There were no women: just men, working in silence. It bothered me, but not quite enough to voice my concerns.

Again, I thought about how perfect this location was if you needed to hold out in a siege, to protect your people. Fear gnawed at my heels, wrapping itself around my shins like an eager feline. I focused on my feet, being careful where I stepped in case the invisible cat tripped me up.

As we approached the building from an acute angle, the workers in the enclosed field began to vanish from my view, but just as the huge side wall of the house obscured them I noted the presence of the occasional armed guard inside the perimeter. Why did workers need guarding like that, and what were they doing outside at night anyway? Or were they in fact slaves? My bad feelings multiplied, turning into genuine trepidation. Despite the fact that the men accompanying us seemed completely at ease, I began to expect the worst. I tried to catch Bob's eye, but he was lost in his own thoughts. I had no doubt that they were similar to mine.

The house was impressive. It was the kind of place I had visited in the past, long ago on school trips and more recently with Kay during weekends away in the country. It had once been a school, I knew that from Bob's description, but it looked to me that even before that it had been some kind of stately home. It was Tudor in design, but with Victorian-era additions to the structure – notably a massive glass-covered front extension filled with potted plants, and additional roof elements which probably housed renovated rooms in the loft space.

From an architectural point of view the building was a mess, but there was no doubt that the space had been utilised to its full potential. I had worked on a few residential homes in the past, redevelopments like this one, and every square foot was worth money to the investors so nothing was wasted in the design.

The glass of the entrance conservatory shimmered as we approached, reflecting the illumination from arc lights set up around the building's perimeter. Most of the building's windows were lighted, which meant that the rooms must be occupied. I saw figures moving past the panes of glass like bulky ghosts. In an upper window, someone pressed the palms of their hands flat against the glass and stared out at us.

A figure emerged from the conservatory doors, dressed in a light green surgical gown, dark green hospital trousers, and heavy army-issue marching boots. He was average height, slight of build, and on his head he wore a ridiculous straw hat, like something you'd see on a Mexican peasant selling beans at the side of a dusty road. The hatband was a dirty red bandana.

"That's Doctor Thwaite," said Wispy, moving ahead of us. Thwaite raised a hand in greeting. He was wearing rubber surgical gloves, which made his hands look as if they had been skinned.

If I had not felt so cautious, I might have laughed.

CHAPTER 17

We were standing in the entrance lobby like guilty children wondering what was expected of us, when the armed guards quietly left our side to return to their posts. Doctor Thwaite had said nothing directly to us, but he had conferred in a hushed manner with Wispy – who was obviously high up in the chain of command – and seemed satisfied with whatever he had been told.

At last, when the final boiler-suited figure closed the door behind him, Thwaite turned to us to fully appraise our shabby gathering. "I'm sorry about all the palaver. We're living in dangerous times." His voice was so normal in both tone and delivery that it was a struggle not to dismiss him as perhaps a tactical stand-in and turn around to look for whoever was really in charge here. The man behind the curtain who controlled the Great and Mighty Oz. The organ grinder making the monkey dance for pennies. "We have to protect what we have here – even if that means offending occasional visitors to our little community." His smile was smooth and easy and perfectly sane, but his appearance was all wrong. It was unclear whether he had lost his mind or found it.

"I came to get my mother. I need to know if she's still here." Bob moved forward, standing in front of me, blocking me off from Thwaite. "Her name's Jessica Willis. She's in room twenty-five, on the second floor." He stared at our host, his gaze unwavering. Beads of sweat had gathered on his brow and upper lip.

Thwaite shook his head and rubbed his gloved hands together. I was almost disappointed that they did not squeak. "I'm sorry – Mr. Willis, is it? By the time I got here, most of the residents and all of the staff were either gone or... *gone*. I'm sorry. All we were able to do was give those who remained a dignified burial."

Bob's shoulders slumped. He lost at least a couple of inches off his height as he moved away from me to occupy his previous position. His gaze turned inward, no doubt seeking memories of his mother.

"Please. Come on through, and let me introduce myself. I'm Doctor Thwaite, and this is my little community." He made an expansive gesture, taking in the interior of the home and everything beyond its walls as we followed him into a huge, beautifully decorated study or reception room.

Outside the large front window, a man was standing facing the darkness. He held a rifle across his broad chest. The room in which we stood was lined with bookshelves along two walls, and oil paintings hung framed beneath spotlights on the third, adjacent to the window. It was a nice room – a gorgeous room, if I'm honest – but it held somewhere within its walls a form of mute horror that I was unable to locate in terms of real time and space. As if the screams of the people who had died here were tattooed on the walls, pressed beneath the carpets, and held like stains in the narrow grain of the woodwork.

"My name's Mackenzie Booth," I said, turning away from the window and feeling a ghostly chill deep within my bones. "This is Bob Willis, and my other two friends are Becky Talbot and Manisa Sahib."

"I'm glad to know you. Please, sit down. I seem to have forgotten my manners in all the fuss. You'll have to forgive me, we're not very organised yet, still trying to get things in order. Could I offer you some drinks?" He walked to a teak drinks cabinet and started to pour whisky from a decanter into five glasses. "Decent stuff, a fifteen year-old malt." Again I wondered if the man's mind had begun to disintegrate during recent events or if he had in fact discovered deep within himself a crystalline form of sanity that cut through the surface concerns of society to focus on what really mattered – the task of survival, and rebuilding what was left after a great fall from grace.

"Thanks," I said, accepting the whisky a little too eagerly. I drank quickly, enjoying the burn as the spirit made its way down my throat and into the empty pit of my belly. I wished that he'd offer us some food. Thwaite refilled my glass without me having to ask. If it were not for the comedy Mexican hat, creased surgical attire and rubber gloves, I would have believed that he was simply managing his people in a crisis. But all these things pointed to a possible derangement of his character which rendered his other actions deeply suspect. Despite my previous thoughts, I decided that he was either mad before all this happened, or had made a quick transition to madness.

"Over the past twenty-four hours we've secured this area and got to work preparing for an unstable future. Over half the population has gone – and this is all from the official figures, before the lines of communication went down. I'd guess the numbers are even higher than that. Those of us left need to band together to fight the other ones, the ones who are hell-bent on murder and suicide." His rubber hands gripped his glass. His eyes were wide and steady, betraying nothing of what was going on behind them. "I assume you understand what I'm talking about?" The silence after his last word seemed unfathomable.

"Leftovers," said Becky, touching me in such an obscure way that I was almost moved to tears.

"Yes." Thwaite sipped his whisky. "That's the name which seems to have stuck. I suppose it's as good as any; although personally I'm not really taken with it. Some things shouldn't have names."

"So," I interrupted. "You're a medical man, a doctor? What's your professional theory on all this?"

Manisa sat down on a leather sofa, stretching out her legs. Becky crossed to the window, glancing outside as the man with the rifle moved slowly away and stepped across the lawn, heading towards another group of men who were erecting some sort of wooden structure over by the fence, similar to the ones I'd noticed along the outer perimeter when we'd arrived. Bob just stood there in the middle of the room, adding nothing to the discussion. His gaze was now frozen on the floor at his feet, but I knew that what he saw was his mother's face in the busy pattern and weave.

"It's difficult," said Thwaite, taking a chair by the window. "But you're right; I do have a theory, of sorts. It seems to me that mankind has always possessed a sort of built-in obsoletion factor, a sell-by date, if you will. I think that critical date has now been reached, and a switch has flipped inside the human mind – or even the soul, if that's what you prefer to believe." He was warming to his theme; I could see it in his shiny face, in his dull insect eyes.

"And that's why this is all happening? The suicides, the killing. All of it. Because of this genetic sell-by factor?"

Thwaite nodded. "In general terms, yes. It isn't that simple, of course, but I think that perhaps a previously buried common genome, or a certain biological trigger embedded in the jigsaw of human DNA, has suddenly come into play, causing all this madness and chaos. It's an Extinction Level Event: the possible end of our species. It might even have been pre-programmed since the beginning of the evolutionary process, like a computer virus embedded in an ageing hard drive."

Bob laughed suddenly. Just the once, like a single bark from a mad dog. He did not repeat the sound.

Thwaite blinked, shook his head. "They're dead, you know."

It took me several seconds to bring myself back into the room, to once again fully occupy the moment and engage with the man. "I'm sorry? *Dead*? Who's dead?"

"Your leftovers... those marauding destructors. They're dead, all of them. I've already examined a corpse some of my militia managed to drag back here, to my lab. The body was fresh – the leftover threw himself in front of one of the vans – but the brain had been dead for hours. *Hours*."

My head began to throb. The pain was good; it meant that I was still here, and not dreaming. After all, you don't hurt in your sleep; you don't ache in your nightmares. "You're telling me that those things are already dead, like... well, like zombies from some stupid horror film? Come on, *doctor*." My emphasis on this last word was entirely deliberate. Thwaite either failed to notice or chose not to react to my intended slight.

"I believe in facts, and the facts tell me that they are dead, but still moving, still active, and even still conscious. They have a rudimentary form of intelligence, enough to get together in groups and hunt down survivors – even to communicate with each other at a very basic level. Have you seen what they do to themselves? The bloody disfigurements. Those terrible acts of self-mutilation? I think that's a way of staving off the suicidal urge – the physical trauma from their wounds keeps the urge back, under control, at least for a little while... until they can find others to kill as they destroy themselves. Like some strange delayed kamikaze syndrome – you know; the Japanese fighter pilots during the Second World War? That's what I like to call it, this phenomenon: the Kamikaze Syndrome." He smiled; he actually grinned, so very pleased with himself.

I slumped onto the sofa next to Manisa. She reached out and grabbed my hand. Her fingers were cold, yet her skin was silk-smooth, whisper-soft. It felt as if I was holding on to strands of cloud.

Thwaite stood, surveying the room. It was as if he were performing, acting out a role for us all to enjoy. "They're not alive, and they're not quite dead – certainly not in the sense that we would use the word. They are both more and less than your silly movie zombies. They have *become* Death." His cheeks shone in the low light; his eyes were flat and dull, like plastic balls sunk into his head. But he was still smiling; he was enjoying this. All of it. I almost expected him to stop and signal for applause.

I glanced out of the window, at the militia struggling with their framework at the fence line. It looked as if they were assembling it in order to carry it outside the gate, and as I watched that's exactly what happened. They had mounted the thing on a little wooden dolly, and pushed and pulled it through the open gate. I watched for a while longer, until they had vanished into the darkness. The stars were weak and indistinct above the spot where they had been; the moon was a lightly sketched outline against the brilliant blackness of the night sky.

"Sir." Wispy had entered the study. I did not even hear him open the door. "The guest rooms are ready." He turned around and exited, leaving the door ajar.

Thwaite smiled. "I'm sure you're all very tired. If you'll follow Mr. Tallow here, he'll lead you to your rooms. Please feel free to wander the house at will, but I'd advise strongly against leaving the premises and walking around outside. Leftovers have been spotted nearby, and we're expecting some kind of attack."

"Is that the reason for the armed guards?" I stood, reached down to help Manisa to her feet. "To fight off an attack?"

"Oh, there's always a good reason for armed guards, Mr. Booth. Let me assure you of that." His smile was empty, dead, devoid of even a suggestion of humanity. "Always a *very* good reason."

Tallow barely spoke as we followed him up the wide, curving staircase to the first floor. He called out our individual rooms as we reached them, like a soldier carrying out a roll-call. Bob's was the first door on the landing, then a few doors along Tallow pointed out Becky's quarters, and finally Manisa's room was located next door to mine. None of us went inside, yet Tallow waited as if he expected us to do so. After a few seconds, he turned away and went back downstairs, where I heard murmured voices drifting in the still, dusty air of the house.

"This is fucking weird." Becky stood hugging herself, as if she were cold. "This bloke's building a private army. I think we should leave. Like, now."

Manisa shook her head. "If we do leave, I think it should wait until morning. We don't seem to be in any immediate danger, but Thwaite strictly expressed that we shouldn't go walking around outside. I think we should respect that warning. There are idiots with guns out there, and if they think they've spotted a leftover they'll just shoot you first and ask your name later."

I took a deep breath. "What do you think, Bob?"

He twitched, looking up from the floor as if waking from a light snooze. "I'm sorry... yes, I think we should stay. Get some rest. We can leave in the morning. I know he said everyone was gone or dead, but I want to be certain that my mother isn't here. I'll be checking out the upper floors once things quieten down. If anyone wants to join me..."

"Count me in," I said, if only to humour him. "Once we're settled, I'll meet you back out here. Say in an hour?"

"So that's it, then?" Becky seemed angry at being outvoted, but there was little I could do to reassure her. "We're staying?"

"It might be the wisest move," I said, trying to sound sympathetic. "Just for the night. Believe me, I want to get away as soon as I can. My wife..."

Becky's features softened. "Yeah. Okay. But I'm barricading my fucking door and I'm not coming out until daylight."

"Good idea," said Bob. "I might just do the same. After I check for any sign of Mum."

There didn't seem much else to discuss, so I opened the door to my room and glanced inside. "Cosy," I said, feeling rather stupid for doing so. "An hour, Bob."

"See you then," he said, quietly – too quietly, I thought – and drifted back along the hall to his own room.

"See you in the morning," said Becky, and she retreated into her room. I heard the sound of a heavy item of furniture being moved across the floor, and a gentle thud as she shifted it into position on the other side of the door.

"Night, then," said Manisa, looking down; then her gaze moved up my body, from my feet to my face. Her eyes were huge in the dimness of the landing. They glowed like embers. Somewhere in the house, timber creaked; hushed voices drifted up the stairwell; something heavy fell to the floor in another room – perhaps even Becky's.

My throat was dry; my lips felt like they were about to crumble to dust. "Goodnight." I turned away, feeling hot and anxious and on the verge of something that I could never take back, not if I let it overpower me and force my hand. "Goodnight." I closed my door, not daring to look over my shoulder, and left her standing there in the shadows. As far as I remember she stood there for a while longer before moving away; eventually I heard her soft footfalls on the boards, and I turned and pressed my forehead hard against the door as they slowly faded from earshot.

No, I thought. *Don't do it.* My hand strayed to the door handle. I gripped it tightly, wanting to turn it and throw the door wide. But instead I just held it, held it, and waited for the moment to pass. They always do, such moments, if you're strong enough to outwait them, to allow them to wash over you and through you and wear a layer of skin off your body.

CHAPTER 18

I was lying on my back with my hands clasped behind my head when I heard a gentle knocking at my door. It was not exactly predictable, but nor was it completely unexpected. I sat up on the bed, feeling the thick mattress shifting slightly beneath me, and listened. The sound came again: a gentle rapping, as if by a small hand…a *woman's* hand.

I considered ignoring it and burying my face in the pillows, but I knew that if I did so there was a slim chance that I might be putting whoever this was in some kind of danger. *Whoever this was…*I knew exactly who it was, and she *knew* that I knew. It was her: Manisa. Of course it was. It could not possibly be anyone else.

My mobile phone was on the bed, the battery finally spent. I'd tried to call or text Kay as soon as I entered the room, but despite a momentary flaring on the screen as I punched the appropriate button, the phone had abruptly turned itself off. I did not have a battery charger on me, but I thought there must be one somewhere in the house. A place this size, which had contained so many people, must surely be filled with useful stuff and I'd already established the electricity supply was in working order.

We cling to such hopes in times of crisis: they sustain us, like a drowning man grasping at sticks in the water. But like those sticks, their promise often proves false and they quickly fall apart.

The room was decorated with subtly patterned wallpaper and there was a picture rail running along the top of the walls, a foot or so beneath the high ceiling. The furniture was old, but not antique – just used items placed together in a rough approximation of taste. I guessed that a resident had stayed here rather than a member of staff, as it seemed to have been designed with an eye for comfort rather than utilitarianism. There were blank patches on the walls, carved out of the light layer of dust, where pictures had once hung. Thwaite and his men must not have had the time to rearrange the rooms – nor would they have had any reason to do so – so I suspected that someone might have died in the room prior to the world tipping on its axis, and the space had been cleared in preparation for the next resident to move in.

She knocked a third time, gently insistent, not going away. The sound hung in the air like particles of shed skin held in a breeze.

I disengaged my mind from the décor and got to my feet. My shoes lay on the floor at the foot of the bed, where I'd kicked them off in my haste to relax, but I did not pause to put them back on. Instead I crossed the room and stood at the door, placing the tips of my fingers gently against the wooden panel. "Hello?" My feet felt impossibly vulnerable.

"Mack. It's me, Manisa." Her voice was not much more than a whisper.

"I know. I can't let you in."

"Why not? It's cold out here. *Really* cold."

"No it isn't. I can't... please, don't make me let you in. Don't *let* me let you in." I closed my eyes and tried to picture my wife's face, but I could not summon her features from the buzzing darkness gathering behind my lids. I imagined how our unborn child, the one we self-consciously called He-She, might look in a few years time, but once again my inner vision failed and all I saw was the outline of a child who might have belonged to anyone – a total stranger forming from shadow inside my head.

"Let me in, Mack."

"No. I can't." But my hand crept to the door handle, and turned it slowly, oh so slowly, making it click loudly in the bulky silence. My ears pricked; my skin was moist. I licked my lips but no spit came. "No."

I opened the door.

No. This time I did not even say the word, just thought it; a mental whisper.

She stood there, in her bare feet and her long sweater, with nothing covering her slim, brown legs. "I got lonely," she said, taking a step inside – and, like a vampire, once invited she claimed the territory as her own, making her mark, leaving her scent.

Her lovely scent.

"Lonely." I echoed the word, tasting its resonance like spice on my dry tongue, feeling it smudge against my aching teeth. "Lonely." And God how I knew what she meant, how she felt. Because I was lonely, too: lonelier than I could ever have imagined – or even explained. Certainly more lonely than I would have admitted. This girl, this pretty young thing with her small hands and her soft, brown skin, would never be able to contemplate the depth of my loneliness, not even if she tried to do so for as long as she lived.

Lonely.

I closed the door, taking a single step backwards, moving quickly away from her – and as far as I could from the dense shadow of my own desire. But it was not far enough, never quite far enough to make a difference.

"I got scared." She closed the door behind her. Her legs were bare. "I heard noises. Voices. Footsteps. Somebody stopped outside my door and laughed before moving on."

Her legs were bare.

She walked nimbly towards me, as if pulled by a silken thread. Her body moved with grace and a natural athleticism that I had not allowed myself to acknowledge until now. "I'm sorry for coming here, to your room, but where else could I go? Becky's barricaded herself in... Bob's, well, he's a little intense."

"And me?"

Her legs were bare.

"You're a nice guy, and nice guys are in short supply right now." She flicked her dark, blue-tinted fringe of hair off her forehead with slim, strong fingers; her eyes were dark and deep and mystifying.

"I'm married, Manisa... my wife's waiting for me." My voice sounded so unconvincing that I could have been reciting lines from a script, something written years ago, when all those people were still alive and long before the nightmare had begun. "Come on, let's not get into something we might both regret. Let's not..."

"I don't believe in regrets."

(Her legs were bare)

"Regrets are for losers."

I simply did not know how to reply to that. Her face swam towards me in the dim room, a shark moving in for the kill. But I was a willing victim – not a victim at all, not really. In reality, we were both assuming and enjoying the role of the hunter, circling each other in shallow waters and waiting for the inevitable first strike.

"Come here." She stood before me, a vision that I did not want to witness but found impossible to deny. Her beauty was ragged, tired, yet it held a grimy glamour beyond anything I had ever experienced. In that moment she became the ultimate women; the only woman. And I was the only man.

We were the only couple.

I stepped towards her, knowing that I was lost – that I had been lost since the moment she noticed me.

Her legs...

...were bare...

It is irrelevant to note who instigated the first kiss. We were both hungering for this act, and ridiculous notions of blame were cast aside, thrown to the floor along with her sweater and my trousers. Her skin was immaculate; the downy hairs on her arms stood up as if prickled by static electricity. The energy that fizzed between us seemed simultaneously base and utterly transcendental. The moment was special, almost spiritual, but it was also absurdly banal and rooted in the muck of the earth, like a piece of poetry suddenly uttered by an insect.

She was very thin, petite, but her breasts were slightly too large for her frame. Her lean legs wrapped around me, tightening against my waist as we fell back onto the bed. I cannot even remember how we made the transition from being partially clothed to entirely naked. It was as if our remaining clothes came apart at the seams, and they peeled as easily as orange skin from our bodies.

We did not make love; not that. We simply fucked, but we fucked like true lovers. It was hard, desperate, as if by my penetrating her we might both reach the key to some kind of inner sanctuary located deep within the entrance to her womb.

She whispered harshly into my ear, but I could not make out the meaning: it was a language all of her own, guttural and utterly improvised. Fictional words and phrases whose sense I understood without being able to discern what they actually meant. The entire act was a contradiction, yet it also felt so terribly natural. I did not think of my wife even once during our time together, not even afterwards, as we lay there damp and steaming and panting like dogs, our eyes turned to the ceiling and our hearts hammering like little machines in the housing of our chests.

My left hand was resting on Manisa's bony pelvis, my fingers tracing the firm curve of her pubis. I made tiny rings in the hair, responding once again to its texture. "I'm not going to say anything that might ruin the moment."

She turned to me, smiling. Her teeth were unbearably white; her hair was a mess, the blue streaks looked like they had spread into the rest of her unruly tresses. "Good. Let's just leave it at that. Everything's different now. Our lives have been split into separate parts. Your wife doesn't even exist in this fragment."

Although self-serving, I could see the logic in what she was trying to say. As Bob said earlier, the rules had changed now. Nothing was left unaltered. This time spent with Manisa could be put into a box and locked away, kept compartmentalised. Again, I was seeking control, imposing my will on the situation, but if this meant that I could deal with what had just happened then I would go along with it. My mind was the best weapon I had, and even the slightest pangs of regret might affect its workings.

"What time is it? You need to meet Bob. It's better if he doesn't go off alone. He might do something... silly." She was leaning on one elbow, her breasts sagging in a wonderfully human way, the large, dark nipples like inquisitive eyes peering at me in the night. Her belly was smooth, yet soft, and I rejoiced in its wholly natural beauty.

"You're right. I should go. Wait for me here?" I could not believe what I was asking, and worse still was the fact that no guilt accompanied the request. I had successfully boxed off this chapter of my life, and I genuinely believed that everything else could remain unaffected by my actions. Now, after everything that followed, I cannot forgive myself for being so blasé and arrogant. Everything in life is connected; we cannot possibly prevent leakage from one event to the next. Each thing that happens is another link in the eternal chain of cause and effect.

But back then, in my willing ignorance, I needed it all to be separated, like snapshots placed inside shoe boxes, each neatly labelled with the year and the name of the event to which it belonged.

"I might be here when you get back. But then again, I might not. No promises, Mack. Not now; not ever. Promises are from the past, before all of this. It's different now. It's all changed." She parted her legs, then swung them around and sat up, her back arching in a smooth brown parabola. The insides of her thighs were slick with sweat. The blue in her hair had turned to black; everything about her was dark, forbidden. "Emotions are taboo." Her voice was nectar; the sight of her sustained me.

I reached out to touch her but she pulled away, laughing softly and rolling onto her back. "Later," she said, inching across the mattress to perch on the edge of the bed, the soles of her oddly long feet now touching the carpet. "Maybe. Now go and see Bob. Keep him from doing something that might get us all into trouble."

I stood and got dressed, watching Manisa in the mirror. She stared at me in the darkness, her lips slightly parted and her eyes as wide as the world. She was stroking her hair, rearranging it carefully so that it looked neater. She seemed much more relaxed than before, and I had certainly felt a subtle shift within me, as if the pressure of our situation had lifted enough to allow me to see more clearly what we needed to do.

I crossed the room and opened the door just a crack, peering out onto the landing. It was dark and empty, the lights had been extinguished. Somewhere a clock ticked; the building settled noisily. I glanced back at Manisa on the bed, but she had reposed and pulled the covers over her lower torso. Her skin shone like oil. Her hair was a vague blue-black spill across the flat white pillow.

Remembering to breathe, trying not to scream, I opened the door fully and stepped out onto the landing. Bob was not there, but I knew that he wouldn't keep me waiting for long. I stood in the quiet and the dark, thinking about what had just happened, and wishing that I was able to feel even a smidgeon of regret.

Already this felt like a dream, or like another part of this ongoing dream in which I found myself trapped.

I looked at my hands, remembering what they had just been doing. I could taste Manisa in my mouth. I still felt the memory of her heat on my skin and her strange spiced scent lingered wilfully in my nostrils. Thoughts of Kay and He-She could not have been further from my mind.

CHAPTER 19

"Is there a television in your room?"

Bob's voice took me by surprise and pulled me out of the cage of my thoughts. He seemed more in tune with our surroundings than before, as if he had somehow regained his focus. "No," I said. "There isn't. At least not that I've noticed."

"Come with me, then. You need to see this." He paced back along the landing, to his door, and waited for me there. The door was open and pale silvery light spilled out onto the landing at our feet. "Get ready for some serious weirdness." He pushed open the door and walked inside.

I followed reluctantly, feeling as if something in Bob had changed. He no longer seemed to be the calming presence I'd grown accustomed to; there was a new hardness to his demeanour that chilled me. "What is it, mate? I don't understand."

"You will." He stepped to the side, allowing me to see the interior of the room. His bedclothes were creased, where he'd been lying down, and the pillows had been bunched up against the headboard. The television was on, but there was no programme running on the screen.

Instead there were words: simple, bold font, white on black.

I looked at Bob. He nodded. "Like I said: serious weirdness."

I looked back at the screen, trying to take it all in. My eyes began to water and my head throbbed. The words, however, remained burned into my vision.

IT WAS THEM

I remembered the words we'd seen painted on the bridge alongside the suicides, and then the text messages on every phone we had in our possession. These words were slightly different, but their meaning was the same.

"Who do you think is sending them? The messages. Is it Thwaite?"

Bob sat down on the bed. "I doubt it. How could he send the same text to every mobile phone? This is worse than that. It's verging on the fucking paranormal, man."

"Come on; let's not get carried away here. I don't believe in ghosts."
I sat down next to him. There was no warmth coming from his body.

"Neither do I, but I *do* believe that something unnatural is
happening, something unexplainable in normal scientific terms. You
have to admit that none of this makes any sense whatsoever, not in the
rational way we're used to thinking." He turned and stared at me. His
eyes were heavy-lidded; there were black circles etched in the skin
around them. "It isn't natural. Not right."

We both turned our attention back to the television screen at the
same time, which meant that we both saw the words change. It
happened smoothly, without any kind of interference or static. Nothing
altered except the message.

THEY KILLED YOUR CHILDREN

"Do you believe me now?" Bob's voice was far too calm, much too
restrained to make sense in the situation. He should have been terrified
– at least as afraid as I was right then – but all that I sensed from him
was a strange calm acceptance.

THEY TORTURED YOUR PARENTS

The words changed again, appearing for only a few seconds before
being replaced by another message, or a continuation of the same
message.

THEY RAPED YOUR WIVES
THEY CASTRATED YOUR HUSBANDS
THEY ENDED YOUR LIVES
THEY DID IT

Then the loop repeated, over and over again. We watched it go
through several repetitions of the same chilling statements before Bob
calmly stood, reached out, and turned off the television.

"I can't believe this. I just… I can't."

"Believe it." His voice was steady, unflinching. "Accept it. Things
have gone haywire. Nothing you ever believed in exists anymore. No
God, no religion, no humanity. Just this damned message, and the

emptiness behind it. There's no man in a studio pumping out this stuff, it's just appearing, like an echo of what we're all thinking and have been thinking for a long time. It's a fucking primal scream, a cry for help that's been heard far too late to make a difference." He bowed his head. It took me a while to realise that he was crying. He made no sound; no tears stained his cheeks. But he was crying.

"Bob?" I reached for him, grabbing his forearm.

"It's crazy... fucking crazy." He raised his arm and showed me his watch. It was digital, very high-tech and with a tiny screen, and on that screen were the same words, scrolling like a miniature teletype giving football updates on match day. Bob struggled to remove the watch, but his hands were shaking too much to undo the strap. At least he was showing emotion, breaking down like the rest of us. I helped him with the watch and he threw it to the floor. Then he stood up and stamped on it, his mouth closed, jaw locked.

"Are you okay?"

He stopped stamping on the watch. "I am now. Let's go and see if my mother's really gone." His face relaxed, and I caught a glimpse of the old Bob again – at least the one I'd known for such a short time. It crossed my mind then that none of our little group really knew each other at all. We had been drawn together by circumstance, and terror had acted as a glue to bind us. Soon the cracks would appear; unseen conflicts would begin to tear us apart.

"Wait." Bob took a torch from the top of the drawers at the side of the bed. He turned it on and smiled. "We don't know what we might meet in the dark."

We left the room, closing the door behind us, and walked slowly along the landing to the stairs. Peering down the staircase, we waited to see if there was any movement elsewhere in the house. Somewhere a door slammed; footsteps sounded way up on one of the upper floors. Music drifted from somewhere I could not locate, but it was very faint – perhaps someone was playing a record downstairs, in a room at the rear of the house.

"Come on." Bob touched my arm. I glanced at him, and he nodded. "Up." He pointed the torch beam at the ceiling.

I followed him up the stairs to the next level, where he knew his mother's room was located. At the top of the flight we peered along the next landing.

"*Twenty-five.*" Bob mouthed the number silently. I pointed along the landing. He nodded again, and then trotted quietly across the carpet. All of the doors were shut, but light bled under one or two of them.

We reached the room in seconds. Fear tickled my face and neck like dangling cobwebs and I couldn't shake the feeling that we were being watched.

Bob stood outside the door, holding the handle. He was staring at the wood, as if attempting to see through it and into the room beyond. The torch was pointed at the floor when he turned it off. I waited for him to gather himself, not wanting to startle him out of whatever trance he had entered. At last he blinked, shuffled his feet, and turned the handle.

The door was unlocked. It opened smoothly and easily, onto darkness. I could make out the separate shapes of furniture inside the room – a low bed, a wardrobe pushed against the wall, a couple of armchairs, what must have been a dressing table. I looked back at the bed, my gaze drawn by something I did not fully understand. Then, a little late, my brain kicked in and caught up with my eyes, and I realised that there was someone lying on the bed: a vague lumpy shape beneath the covers in the gloom.

I grabbed Bob's shoulder. He slipped his hand over mine, prised apart my fingers, and pushed the torch into my hand. He was strong – much stronger than I had first thought. I hoped that strength was mental as well as physical. He might need it if that was his mother's corpse on the bed.

I let Bob enter the room before I followed, drawing the door quietly towards the frame as I did so. I did not shut it fully, but left it ajar. I'm not sure why – there was no illumination coming in through the gap from the landing– but it felt like the right thing to do. Perhaps it was a subconscious act, allowing for the promise of a speedy escape.

Bob approached the bed. He moved silently, like a ghost. His outline was stark against the wall, and despite being unable to discern his features I knew that he was bunching the muscles in his jaw and setting his face into a tough mask for what was to come. He reached the end of the bed, moved around it, and stood above the silent figure. Then, just as he began to lift his hand away from waist level, the body moved, turning onto its side.

It was not Bob's mother.

I stumbled slightly in shock as I tried to switch on the torch, and my foot caught the door, making a slight noise. The figure moved again, turning and trying to sit up. It mumbled. Bob acted quickly, reaching out and grabbing it by the throat. He stood there, squeezing, and as the figure thrashed on the bed he leaned into it, forcing his body weight on top of the struggling body and smothering it. He never lost his grip; his large hands were shaking as his thick fingers squeezed.

It took a long time for the figure to stop moving, and I just stood there, rooted by fear and shock and a sense of disbelief, pointing the torch beam at what was taking place on the bed. When someone is strangled in films or on TV, it seems like such a simple and effortless affair, but this took ages and involved a lot of effort. The figure tried its best to fight back, but Bob had the advantage because of his position and the fact that he already had hold of the figure's neck. The sounds it made were horrible: wet, choking, gasping noises, like nothing I had ever heard before. When finally the figure went limp, Bob stepped away from the bed. He was panting for breath. His whole body was shaking.

I was shaking, too. With fear.

Finally I found my voice. "Shit, Bob. Why did you do that?"

He loomed in the torchlight, suddenly bigger than before. "I... I don't know. I think they killed her. My mum. None of this is right. It's like a prison or a concentration camp" He slumped against the wall, the shaking subsiding. Then he raised his hands and clutched at his face, his head.

"Quickly," I said, desperate to take charge of the situation. "We have to hide the body." I stepped across the room and looked down at the dead man – it *was* a man, one of Thwaite's soldiers by the look of him. There was a boiler suit folded up on one of the chairs, and a shotgun stood in one corner, propped against the wall. I balanced the torch on the bed so that we had light to work by.

We managed to move the body and put it on the floor next to the large wardrobe. I opened the doors and was thankful that the wardrobe was empty but for a few dresses hanging like old, discarded skins.

"Mum's," said Bob, his voice weak and watery. "They're Mum's..."

I took the dresses and their hangers and slid them under the bed, where no one would see them. Then, with great effort, Bob and I manhandled the body into a more or less upright position inside the wardrobe. One of us knocked the torch off the bed, and it rolled across the floor, the light jittery and restless. The man's feet were sticking out of the wardrobe, preventing me from closing the door, and it took us quite some time to manoeuvre them so that they stayed inside. I closed the door, leaning against it. The wardrobe was the old-fashioned kind, constructed of sturdy timber and with a key to lock it. I turned the key, my hands slippery and shaking. Then, feeling sick and light-headed, I pushed away from the wardrobe and stared at Bob. I put the wardrobe key in my pocket and picked up the torch.

"I'm sorry..."

"You fucking idiot." I was surprised at the anger in my hushed voice. "When they find him, they'll kill us. All we had to do was keep our heads down, get some sleep, and then leave peacefully in the morning. That was it, fucking simple. But you had to go and fuck it up."

"Sorry..." He was like an overgrown child, and suddenly I realised that what I had mistaken as strength of character before was actually an act, a mask he had worn all his life. He was a big man with a soft heart and, although he had been holding on heroically since I'd met him, now his meagre defences were crumbling. Bob was just a big Mummy's Boy whose sanity had snapped to reveal the gaping chasm devoid of genuine character beneath.

"Okay, okay. Let's just get back to our rooms and wake the girls. We have to get out of here. *Now.*" I strode towards the door, opened it, and checked outside. All quiet, all dark, all empty. Nobody had heard us. I could still make out that distant music, and now identified it as classical. I did not recognise the piece, or the composer, but it was definitely some kind of light chamber music. It sounded incongruous under the circumstances, and the urge came upon me to laugh. I swallowed it down, staying in control.

I moved back along the landing, towards the stairs. Bob was behind me. I could sense his unease and something else – something bleaker and far more terrifying. It was as if by killing the man in the room Bob had crossed an invisible line and transformed, becoming a fractured version of the man I thought I knew: a rebooted Bob who was capable of anything.

We descended the stairs in silence, that odd, displaced music still playing downstairs. I hoped it would mask any noise we did make, but for the most part we moved down quickly and carefully, guided by the torch beam. I could hear Bob's breathing behind me; it was heavy, ragged, like that of an asthmatic.

"We meet back here in ten minutes," I said. Bob just stared at me. "Bob! Snap out of it. We have to move."

Bob nodded, but still I was unsure if he had understood.

I left him there, on the landing outside his room, and returned to see if Manisa was still in bed. I opened the door and went inside, noticing immediately that the bed was empty. She must have gone back to her own room, perhaps seeing the error of both our ways. I closed my eyes and breathed deeply, trying to rid myself of the fear that was threatening to take over my senses. This was all too much; everything was spinning out of control. Why the hell had Bob done that? Perhaps, I thought, he had been unhinged all along but I had failed to notice the signs.

The signs?

How the hell would I even recognise the signs of madness? I was an architect not a psychologist. For all I knew, we were all crazy and this entire situation was the product of some kind of group insanity. Were we, even now, lying in hospital beds experiencing the same lucid nightmare? Maybe we'd all enrolled in some experimental drugs programme, and this was all just a weird group hallucination... but no, I could not allow myself to think such things. This was real; I had already established that. To even consider any other option would be to embrace a fantasy.

I checked the room and made sure that I had my mobile phone.

The phone. The dead phone. The urge to call Kay was upon me, and it was stronger than my fear. I still had a few minutes to spare before going back out there, rousing the girls, and trying to get Bob to act in a rational manner. Time enough to make a quick call.

Time to make a call even though the battery was dead.

I handled the mobile handset carefully, as if it might break. I stared at the dead screen, fondled the keys. It was such a short step, really, from here to there. And not much different to anything I had done up to this point: a simple act of pretending, like so much else we were pretending in this twisted new world.

Pretending...

...I keyed in Kay's number and pressed the handset against my ear, listening to nothing but trying to summon the sound of a telephone

Gary McMahon

ringing…
　　…I pressed the handset against my ear and pretended…
　　…I pretended and then I heard…
　　…I heard the sound of the phone ringing.
　　I spoke:
　　"Hello, Kay."

CHAPTER 20

— *Hello, Kay.*

— *Oh, thank God. Are you safe? Are you well? Where the hell are you?*

— *It's okay, darling. I'm fine. We're stuck in this crazy place – a rest home – but we're just about to leave. Not long now. Not long before we're together.*

— *He-She has been kicking. We miss you.*

— *Not too long now, baby. Not long...*

— *You sound weird... different. Has something happened?*

— *I could never hide from you, could I? You always did see right through me.*

— *Because I love you so much. We're a team, remember. You and me against the world.*

— *And there's He-She, now. Don't forget He-She.*

— *How could I?*

Something... something has happened, but I'm not sure I want to tell you what it is.

— *No secrets, remember? We made that promise a long time ago. No secrets between you and me. We tell each other everything, even the bad stuff. Even the stuff that hurts.*

— *Everything. No secrets.*

— *So tell me. Tell me what happened.*

— *What I've done.*

— *So tell me what you've done.*

— *I can't.*

— *Tell me.*

— *It'll hurt.*

— *We all hurt. Things are gone now – happiness is gone. We all hurt, but at least we can be honest with each other. Tell me. I have to know.*

— *I slept with someone. A girl, part of our group. I slept with her and I feel like I want to die.*

— *Don't say that. Not ever that. So you slept with her. Big deal. Things are different now. The rules... the rules have all changed. Have I already said that? It sounds like I did? Or somebody did.*

— *No. Somebody else did. I'm getting you mixed up. You wouldn't really forgive me this easily, not in real life.*

— *This isn't real life. It's all in your head. So I do forgive you. I love you and I hate you and I forgive you for sleeping with Manisa. That's such a nice name...*

— *I'm sorry.*

— *So am I. I'm really sorry...*

— *Sorry? For what? It's me who's done this. You have nothing to be sorry for.*

— *Oh, but I do. You know I do. We all have things to be sorry for, but I never got the chance to say it. I didn't have time.*

— *You'll have time when you see me.*

— *Will I?*

— *I'll make time. I'll turn it backwards.*

— *I wish you could.*

— *I love you.*

— *Remember to say my name. Say my name when you come, so I hear you. It's dark down here. Cold and dark and lonely.*

— *I'll say your name.*

— *You promise? You promise you'll say my name?*

— *I promise. I'll say your name.*

— *Say my name…*

— *Kay? Kay?*

— *I'm sorry.*

CHAPTER 21

"Kay."

My eyes were most with tears, which would not come. My face was dry; my cheeks were dusty. The tears would not fall, no matter how much I wanted them to, or how hard I tried to force them. I was dry, bereft: *they would not come.*

I walked over to the door and paused for a moment, trying to put on a new face, one that was not quite so bleak and loveless. I knew that I should regret what Manisa and I had done – what I had *allowed to happen* – but I couldn't. It had felt anything but wrong. I could still feel her touch, taste her skin, and smell her gritty perfume. Despite what I had said to the imaginary Kay on the dead phone, I felt no regret for making love to this beautiful girl.

All I felt was aroused all over again.

I opened the door and stepped outside. Bob was back – or was he still there, right where I had left him? "Bob." He ignored me, simply staring into empty space ahead of him. His eyes had narrowed; his gaze was unfocused, yet turned inward. "Come on, mate. Let's get our arses out of here. Have you checked the girls' rooms?" Again, he ignored me. He did not even move.

I knocked heavily on Becky's door, and when I did so the door shuddered open an inch or two. I remembered her shifting the furniture inside the room, so was immediately concerned that the door was not only unlocked but free of any blockage. My lips were dry. The air on the landing felt thick and turgid.

"Becky?" I pushed the door wide. The room was in darkness; even in the gloom the bed looked as if it had not been slept in. "Are you there, Becky?" I strained to hear something – anything: a sigh, a breath, a muffled voice – but there was nothing. The room was now untenanted. It felt cold, empty, as if she had never even been in there at all.

Heart jittering in my chest, I moved to Manisa's room. I turned the handle and the door swung silently open. I did not have to look inside to know that she was not there. "Manisa." The words tasted like dust in my mouth; the raw detritus of her passing.

For a moment I considered the possibility that neither woman had even existed – that they were figments of my broken mind. But then I managed to regain control. Now, more than at any other point during my life, control was what mattered.

I turned again to face Bob, but he had not budged. He was still staring at nothing, his arms limp at his sides and his face slack and expressionless. Killing the man in his mother's room had snapped his mind, severing him from reality. Or was it the admission that his mother must surely be dead that had done the damage? Perhaps the only thing driving him forward up until that moment had been the hope that he would see her again.

"Bob, we really have to move. We need to find the girls...." He was blank; a meek shop-window dummy.

Light bled across the floor from behind us, creeping up the stairs. That was when I realised I'd forgotten to bring the torch.

"The womenfolk are fine, Mr. Booth. Mack. They're alive and well."

I turned slowly, recognising the voice. Lamplight flickered behind a figure. Thwaite stood at the head of the stairs, once again wearing that stupid Sombrero. This time he had paired it with some kind of muumuu: a long, baggy, white gown that made him look like a cult leader from a low budget Hollywood thriller. "What have you done with them?"

He stepped to the side, the ridiculous gown swaying around his thin legs. Somebody turned on the landing light and its sudden brightness hurt my eyes. "Mr. Tallow has taken them downstairs. They'll be safe there, with the other breeders." His face was blurred, as if I was looking at it through some kind of atmospheric effect. I blinked several times to clear my vision, and gradually his features came back into focus. I wished that I had not bothered; his smile was hideous and empty and yet as sharp as a box of knives.

"If you hurt them, either of them..."

"What? You'll kill me? Oh, don't be so bloody melodramatic, Mack. You're no action hero, just a man, an ordinary man whose pride is being stamped on by a guy in a dress. One wrong move and I'll have you shot." The two men behind him – Tallow and another, slightly older figure– brandished their weapons. Tallow was holding a rifle; the other bloke had a rather old-fashioned looking shotgun. It was too big for him, as if he was just a kid playing with his father's possessions.

Bob chose that exact moment to return to us. It was a bad choice; a *very* bad choice. He moved forward, surprisingly swift and nimble for such a big man who had only moments earlier been locked up inside his own soundlessly fracturing mind. "Bastard," he said. It was his last word, the expletive he bowed out with.

The blast of the shotgun was almost deafening in such a confined space, and the power of the detonation flung Bob backwards, against the wall, his arms wind-milling wildly like those of an inexperienced fighter in a pub brawl. His mouth hung open, teeth bared. His stomach looked like someone had thrown chopped liver at him. The blood had splashed me as he flew by, warm and wet and sticky.

In what felt like less than a second later, Bob was lying on the floor twitching. Blood was still flowing from his wounds; the shotgun pellets had turned a good percentage of his midriff region to mush. I felt sick. My eyes began to water.

"That's a warning," said Thwaite. I stood up straight and stared at him. He was grinning. "Do as you're told or you'll get the same. The women are valuable to us for breeding purposes, but you're just a potential worker." He had all the emotional connection to the moment of a man talking about cattle. Then I realised that was exactly what we were to him: livestock, a way of repopulating the area via his cosy little community.

"Take him to the Gulag." Thwaite's words bit into me, making me wince.

The Gulag... I could only imagine what that might mean.

Tallow grabbed me roughly by the arm and pushed me towards the stairs. Thwaite followed close behind. I dragged my feet, but he kicked the back of my legs, forcing me to move faster. He coerced me down the flight of stairs and out through the conservatory, where we walked around the building towards the small vegetable patch I'd noticed when we arrived. Nobody was working there now; even the armed guards had retired, their shift now over.

"As I said before, we have to band together. To start again. Those who don't join us willingly will be forced, I'm afraid. The time has come for tough decisions to be made and, in the absence of any surviving semblance of what we used to call officialdom, I've decided to grasp the nettle and take charge." Thwaite's eyes were wide, as if he was experiencing a type of religious rapture. "You see, the others had their chance. *Capitalism* had its chance. But the banks and the businessmen messed it all up, and now *we* have to give it a shot. Socialism might have worked before, but now things are too different, too deranged – and deranged times call for deranged methods. Welcome to the third way: not capitalism, not socialism, but *my* way. The *only* way. I call it Thwaitism.

That was when I knew for certain that he was caught up in some kind of religious delusion. He saw himself as a saviour, the Moses to his people. Even if very few of those people had actually followed him willingly to his promised land, and the rest were there under threat of death.

"Haven't you worked it out yet?" he continued. "You must have seen the messages on the dead computers and TVs. Heard it on the abandoned phone lines? The message changes all the time, but it amounts to the same thing. *They* did it. The banks did it. The businessmen did it. They did it all."

I lunged at him, knowing that I would never reach him. "You're a psycho," I said, tensing myself for a reaction from Tallow, who had grabbed me around the waist.

Thwaite looked shocked. "Of course I am. Only a madman would even try to rebuild things, to reshape the world in his own image. But in madness there lies the potential for greatness."

Thwaite was so caught up in his little god-trip that he failed to see the obvious: that he was destined to fail. This could not work; his low-rent Eden would crumble at the first hint of unrest. Sure, they had guns, but I'd like to bet that the slaves outnumbered the slave masters and they were all ready to revolt.

We passed the border of Thwaite's domain. It all looked different now, as if I were truly seeing beyond the façade he had created: cheap fencing and sandbags hastily erected to keep out the leftovers already sighted in the area. It did not look very secure, probably because of the haste in which it had all been constructed, and even the sight of an occasional armed guard did nothing to persuade me that they could protect the place from a serious assault. There were more rickety wooden platforms on the other side of the fence, just like the one I'd seen being pushed outside earlier that evening. Security lamps had been attached to the frames like gaudy Christmas lights. Nailed to these unstable structures were the limp bodies of leftovers. They had been stripped naked, their self-inflicted wounds exposed to the world, and their heads had been positioned facing towards the tree line. Their dead black eyes watched the trees; their broken jaws were locked open, as if in silent screams. Someone, for whatever reason, had stuffed flowers in their mouths.

"Scarecrows," said Thwaite, noticing that I was inspecting the corpses. "We considered using fakes, but they didn't look right. Now that we have a few real ones they'll hopefully keep the rest at bay, at least until we can properly fortify the grounds." He kept walking as he spoke to me, giving a running commentary on the extent of his domain. He seemed proud of what little he had already achieved. It was laughable. Only the guns made the situation serious – the guns and the cold, humourless fact of Bob's murder.

The Gulag lay ahead. It was a small fenced-in area, guarded by more boiler-suited men. Small portable generators hummed and vibrated. More electric lights were located along the fence line, trailing cables across the dirt. Behind the fences (these ones much higher and sturdier than the shoddy defences around the property) the dark shapes of other men and several tired-looking women lay on the ground or under torn tarpaulin sheets, huddled together like refugees. These, I thought, must be the reluctant workers in Thwaite's little tin-pot dictatorship. Like every fascist leader throughout history, he had a supply of unwilling labour to grease the wheels and build the empire.

He was Mussolini in a muumuu; Hitler in a cocked Sombrero.

"This is where you'll be staying. The Gulag. With the workers. The breeders have much less basic accommodation, but we still like to keep them needy. It means they'll be easier to break." Thwaite stopped at the gate and nodded at one of the guards. Then he turned back to me, staring directly into my eyes. "She'll do well when her time comes… the dark girl. Manisa, isn't it? She's a beauty, that one. Just imagine what her children will look like, especially if I pair her up with the right stud… but only after I've indoctrinated her myself." His smile was monstrous, venal and utterly without remorse.

Tallow pushed me forward. The gate was opened. I turned to face my captors. "I'll get out, you know." Again I could not help but attempt to assert control, to force my will upon the situation. "I'll get out and I'll save them."

Thwaite began to laugh. "Oh, you're great. Really, I love this display of gung-ho aggression." Then he turned on his heels and walked quickly away, discussing something with Tallow, his right-hand man. He had effectively dismissed me; my threats had bounced off him like tennis balls hit against a brick wall.

Someone prodded me with what felt like the muzzle of a rifle, and I stumbled into the enclosure. The gate slammed behind me, and I heard the rattle of chains, the jiggling of keys, as it was locked up tight. I glanced around, looking for somewhere to sit down. Faces stared at me with expressions of hunger; large, frightened eyes took me in, examining me in seconds.

"Welcome to the madhouse," said a deep male voice. Someone else laughed hoarsely.

I sat down against the fence to wait. It was all I could do; my only valid reaction to the situation. But I knew that I would not have to wait long, because the area was ripe for an attack. The leftovers would come – perhaps even this night – and under cover of the ensuing chaos I would make my move and escape, taking the girls with me. That was what I told myself. How I managed to assert a kind of control.

I looked around, ignoring my silent companions, and took in my surroundings. The enclosure covered an area of approximately two hundred feet by three hundred feet, and was pretty much secure. The only exit was the front gate, which was guarded by two armed men, and all the fencing was topped with yet more razor wire – although it was spread pretty thin. A body hung like a rag doll across an area of fence to my rear, legs on the inside, head and shoulders on the outside: the shoddy remains of someone who had tried to escape. They could not even be bothered to dispose of him, and had in all probability left the bloodied corpse there on purpose as a warning to the rest of us.

Then I saw the pit.

It was roughly ten feet square and looked quite deep from where I was sitting. Excavated earth had formed a spoil heap all around the edge. I stood and approached the hole, brushing past other inmates without even so much as a passing comment. There was very little chit-chat; they were all either too tired or shocked or uncaring to speak, even amongst themselves. The occasional whisper reached my ears, but I could not make out any words. Perhaps it was just a sound to fill the emptiness, like actors repeating "Rhubarb" in a crowd scene; or was it someone trying to sing away their fear?

As soon as I got close enough to the pit I began to approximate its depth. Six feet, perhaps more – but at least as deep as a grave. Its sides were rough, as if hastily excavated, and the edges were crumbly. At the bottom of the pit were a tumble of bodies, covered in a thin, white layer of what I assumed must be quicklime. I had read once that the powder stopped bodies from smelling and dry-burned them to speed up the process of decomposition.

Was Bob's mother in there, at the bottom of that pit, her powdered face slack and unseeing? Had they found her dead as Thwaite had claimed, or had these people been killed because they had stood in the way of Thwaite's grand plan to repopulate the building with his own prize collection of studs and breeders?

Turning away, I stumbled and fell to the ground, jarring my arse on the hard-packed earth. Whoever had laughed before did it again. The sound was horrible, like something from a nightmare. This time it did not stop immediately, but went on, a grim and drawn-out sound that made me want to kill its maker.

The lights along the fence dimmed. The sound of the generators seemed marginally quieter than before.

I buried my head in my hands and tried to block everything out, the killing and the bodies and the leftovers. However, when I took my hands away the horror was still there, and I could not tell myself that this was all just part of a long bad dream. In truth, I had passed that point many hours ago, when things began to get really bad. Bob's shooting was like a line drawn under the rest of it, or a full stop at the end of a long sentence: an affirmation that this was all far too real to endure.

Breathing deeply, I forced myself to try and regain control, to think clearly and ruthlessly and wholly without pity or mercy. The first chance I got I had to move fast, and anyone who stood in my way must die. I told myself to think of this like killing a rabid animal, or running down a feral dog in the road. All feelings would need to be put on hold; I had to become cold, tough, and utterly remorseless if I was to survive this.

Say my name...

"Kay," I whispered, shaky and uncertain.

Say my name...

"Manisa."

CHAPTER 22

I must have fallen asleep for a short while, because when I opened my eyes it was still night and there was a lean man with a thin, unshaven face sitting next to me. His eyes were sunken, his cheeks hollow, and he looked like he had not eaten in weeks. That must have been how he always looked; it was too early in proceedings for anyone to have been carved that way by starvation or hardship.

He chuckled; not a nice sound. "How's it going?" His voice was deep, and I recognised it as being that of the solitary laugher I'd already heard twice before. "The name's Randall." He stuck out a hand, so I shook it. "Pleased to make your acquaintance." Once again he let out that awful laugh.

"I'm Mack. How long have you been in here?"

He looked me up and down, rubbing his emaciated face with a skinny, claw-like hand. "I've been here for a day now. I came to this place because it had people. Sadly, the people were Thwaite and his barmy army. They were already in control, and even then had about a dozen people inside this pen."

I smiled and shrugged. He relaxed, his shoulders slumping. "I need to get out of here, Randall. I have to get back to my wife." I stared at his narrow face, looking for a shred of pity and finding instead something which I could not name.

He nodded. "Listen: that's why I came over here. You seem to have caused some kind of upset, so I figured you might be the man to help us. We have a plan. Me and a few of the boys, we're going to make a run for it before things get even worse around here."

It was a cold night, and I hugged myself, trying to keep warm under the open sky. "How do you plan to do that?" The chill penetrated my thin shirt, biting into the flesh beneath.

Randall laughed again. "See that pit? The body pit? I helped dig that, and laid the quicklime. They want us to dig another pit – a bigger one – over by the vegetable patch. They must be expecting more bodies over the next few days, as Thwaite goes into overdrive." His smile was terrible: haggard and hungry and lost.

I stared at him; at his wide eyes and his too-large teeth in his almost skinless face. He was an ugly man, but held within those harsh features I saw a certain kind of truth. Here was a man who could be ruthless – who had been forced to sacrifice part of his humanity to dig a pit and fill it with corpses. "So what's your intention?"

"First light, they're going to come in here as usual, waking us up to work. Me and a couple of the fellas are going to be hiding in there, along the rim of the body pit, pretending that we're dead. We'll jump the bastards, and once we're out of this compound we'll run like hell for the fence."

It didn't sound too convincing a plan, and I told him so.

"Ah," he said, hunkering down, his pointed chin almost touching his pigeon chest. "That's where you come in. If you could cause some kind of diversion, we might be able to grab a gun and shoot the fuckers. That way, we all get out. I may be a bastard, but I'm still human. I don't want to leave any of these boys behind." He threw back his shoulders, then, adopting a posture that fell just short of being dignified. In any other setting, and if he did not look so wrecked, it might have succeeded in that aim.

"So, you want me to start yelling at the guards, or something? Maybe do a little dance? And while they're occupied you just grab one?"

"Yep. That's about the gist of it."

"It's a bit desperate, isn't it? I mean, it's very crude. Even flimsy, if you don't mind me saying." This was gallows humour, and we both knew it. Nothing more, nothing less.

"It's all we have, mate. We're in a desperate situation here, in case you hadn't noticed, and it can only get worse. A few more weeks of this and some of us are probably going to start getting ill, even dying. Then we'll get thrown in the pit, with the rest of them. I want to get out while we still have the strength to fight." He licked his lips; his tongue was dark and thin, like that of a lizard. "If we act together, we have a chance. These jokers aren't even real soldiers, just a bunch of losers who share Thwaite's madness."

"Okay. I can't think of a better plan, so I'm in. If we do this right, it might even work and we won't get killed – at least not all of us." Despite the attempt at humour, I had never felt so low, so close to defeat. "They won't be expecting it." I patted him on the shoulder, showing my support, but inside I felt bleak, like a man clutching at sand

and watching it spill through his fists.

"That's what we figured. The element of surprise." He turned around, motioned into the darkness, and I saw a couple of figures scurry across the dirt on their hands and knees. "A couple of the fellas," said Randall. "They've been watching us."

"Well, that's reassuring." I stared at them as they scuttled away, towards the pit.

"What do you think about the diversion? What will you do?" He leaned forward, eager and hungry.

"Don't worry. I'll think of something."

He nodded again, as if he understood my position completely.

"Where are they keeping the other women?"

He looked away, and then back. The side of his face was dry and rough beneath the stubble. Old acne scars decorated his cheeks, forming a pattern that suggested some kind of design. I glanced away, refusing to countenance such madness. "They're over there," he said, pointing towards the main rest home building. "That's where they keep the good-looking ones. The ugly ones go straight in the pit. There's a sort of wooden trap door at the back of the house that leads down into the cellar. They're being kept in one of the cellar rooms. I've seen it. I had to drag a body out and put it in the pit earlier. One of the potential studs went a bit over the top during his audition." His banal language was even more terrifying than what he was saying, and I felt my stomach tense.

Randall caught my look, sighed. "They've gone mad. They probably already were mad, and this has given them an excuse to stop hiding it."

I agreed with him. Thwaite and his men had thrown off their masks, and underneath they were monsters. A few days ago, some of them might have been office workers, council workers, bin men, tobacconists… seemingly average people going about their business, pretending to be sane. But now the world had suddenly changed, and they could afford to remove their disguises to show what hid there, inside the skin and bones and deep within the cold, grey, spongy matter encased within their grinning skulls.

"Come on," said Randall, standing. His scrawny legs looked like sticks wrapped in rags. "I'll explain in detail."

I followed him across the enclosure. We kept low, not wanting to be seen by the guards, who were standing on the other side of the fence and the lights, chatting and smoking and generally ignoring us. They did not see us as a threat, which was something else that we could use in our favour. We reached the edge of the pit, and I tried not to look inside, at what lay beyond the banked earth. On the opposite side of the gaping hole, two men were crouched facing us. One of them raised a hand in greeting. "Are they the ones from back there, when we were talking?" The two men looked demonic.

Randall waved back at the men. "Yeah. Sorry about that."

"It's fine. Everything's fine. I don't even know how to be offended anymore." It was the truth: the unspoken laws of social dynamics had altered so much that it barely even mattered that the men had probably been willing to beat me if I refused to play along with their ridiculous escape plan.

I watched as the first of the men ducked down and scrabbled into the pit, legs first as he rested his elbows on the top of the embankment at the edge. Soil crumbled and fell away in chunks, but he did not fall. He lowered himself down gently, as if afraid to step too heavily on the bodies down there. Then, after finding his balance, he tiptoed lightly across the carpet of cadavers and found a place on the side of the pit where he could lie down and conceal himself.

"Won't it hurt?" I said. "The lime. It'll burn him."

Randall looked at me. "Of course it'll hurt, if it gets on him, but what other option do we have? I'd rather have burned skin than die here, slowly abused into that pit."

I looked back across the pit, at the other man. His descent was not so graceful, and he stumbled as he attempted to drop. He rolled down into the pit, not making a sound. Then, when he came to rest, he simply crawled across the white-powdered corpses and scrabbled part way back up the opposite face. Then he lay still, curled like a large question mark against the muck.

"So they'll stay there until dawn, when the guards come?"

"Yeah," said Randall, looking nervous now that it was his turn to find a bed for the night. "Not too long now. Promise me you'll be awake when they come. That you'll kick up a fuss."

"I promise. Will anyone else help out?"

He shrugged, his bony shoulders like an injured bird's wings. "I dunno. We only just formulated this plan, and thought it best if we kept quiet about things. Your arrival, and the reaction you seem to have on

Thwaite, made us decide to give it a shot."

"Hardly the Great Escape, is it? I mean, it's all a bit off the cuff."

He smiled. "I never had Steve McQueen's looks." Then, quickly and quietly, he was moving over the edge of the pit. I stayed down on my haunches and watched him as he made his way down the face of the pit and reached a point close to the bottom. He was lithe and agile; I wondered if he'd been a runner or something back in the real world. Despite his fleshless build, he looked like he was in pretty good shape – or had been, before the madness and the suicides and the murders.

I stayed there for quite some time, just watching. None of the three men moved, and it was not long until I forgot where each of them was hidden. I lost sight of them amid the layers of death, and eventually turned away, stumbling across the dirt to find a place to wait until daylight stained the horizon. It would not be long now.

I hoped that Randall was correct; that the guards were indeed planning to start work on another pit so early. If the men were forced to stay down there longer than a few hours, I did not want to see what they might look like when they finally came up for air.

I watched the sky, listening to the subdued chatter of the guards as they intermittently checked the lights and walked the perimeter. Some of the other men – the ones on my side of the fence – had at last begun to speak, and if I tried really hard I could convince myself that everything was normal. Then, when I glanced back in the direction of the pit, the illusion broke slowly apart, and I began to see the cracks forming in the scene.

Control. I had to take control. It was all I had; my best and only weapon against the darkness that threatened to overcome me. I thought about making another pretend call to Kay, and then dismissed the idea as flirting too close to another kind of madness.

Birds cried somewhere to the west, but when I looked I could see only the dark clouds and the distant tree tops. Night seemed to lower, covering us like a sheet – not unlike the one pulled over a dead person as he lies on the mortuary slab.

I felt guilty about it, but my mind kept returning to the time I'd spent with Manisa. I saw her naked form thrashing on the bed, her legs held wide apart, the shine of her juices on her thighs as they caught the meagre light. It had never been so intense with Kay, not even at the beginning of our relationship. Our sex life could never have been called particularly bad, but it had hardly been earth-shattering either. Just... *normal.* With Manisa, however, it was all so different – wild and animalistic – and our passion had torn apart the veil to give me a glimpse of what lay beyond.

Whatever it was that lay beyond even this... beyond the madness and the bloodshed and the fear.

It pained me to admit as much, even to myself, but making love to my wife had become a habit. But with Manisa sex was something frantic and essential, as if my sanity had depended on our brief coupling.

For a moment I thought that perhaps that was true.

CHAPTER 23

I woke without even realising that I had slept, blinking into the cold air and listening to the silence that seemed to drift across the ground like a low-lying mist. I knew where I was: there was no uneasy moment when I felt lost or cast adrift. Randall's plan, along with my own part in it, was right at the forefront of my waking mind. I sat up, rubbing my face. My cheeks felt numb; the blood seemed to have collected there and stopped flowing, causing some kind of swelling.

To the east, the sky was brightening. Not much, just a few smudges of light to signal the arrival of dawn. A lot of my fellow prisoners were asleep; some were awake and staring at the sky, possibly imagining that they were not inside the Gulag but elsewhere with their surviving loved ones. I glanced towards the pit, and thought of the three men stationed there. Was the quicklime starting to burn? Did they feel pain but were unable to cry out in case they were discovered? I paused for a moment to appreciate their bravery and their foolishness; no one else would, so I took it upon myself to mark the moment with at least a contemplative thought for each of them.

I moved along the ground, keeping low, and approached the fence. My timing could not have been better, and I wondered if some inner sense had roused me. Two figures were approaching from the direction of the front of the house – the morning shift, coming to relieve the night guards. They were carrying guns, but loosely at their sides. Both men seemed relaxed, and were even chatting softly as they closed in on the Gulag gate.

Maybe Randall's crazy plan would work after all.

I picked up two large loose stones, which had probably been unearthed during the digging of the pits, and held one in each hand. My fists tightened around the cold hardness. I felt stupid, like a child playing at war. The stones were heavy, with sharp edges. I hoped that they would do the trick. I had been a dead-eye aim in my youth, and my hand-eye coordination was still pretty impressive .I was confident that I could make at least a single shot count.

I heard voices as the new guards spoke with those already stationed at the Gulag's entrance, and then the rattle of keys. After a short while the gate opened, and three of them walked inside. The other guard remained outside, smoking a cigarette and scratching his chest as he stared at the lightening horizon.

Their arrogance would prove to be their undoing. They should have been wary of us, because we wanted them dead. But Thwaite's enormous self-confidence had infected his militia and they barely saw their captives as any kind of threat whatsoever. Bad mistake; hopefully it would prove to be their last.

I waited patiently in the gloom, trying to hide behind the sleeping forms around me. I watched as the guards made their way towards the pit, prodding resting figures with the muzzles of their rifles, laughing softly, and even aiming kicks at the heads of people stirring on the ground to draw grunts from their victims.

I waited, waited… I had to pick my moment, or this would be over before it had even begun. There would be no second chance; I had to hit the target.

Just as they drew level with the edge of the pit, I struck.

I stood quickly, waving my arms in the air. The three guards twitched, instantly alarmed, but none of them raised their gun. There was no real method to my actions; I simply wanted to stun them, to buy some time and cause a ruckus. I threw the stones fast and hard, aiming for their heads. I got one of them in the chin with the first shot, and he went down onto one knee, flailing at his bloody face with a gloved hand. The other two finally realised that they were under attack and brandished their weapons awkwardly, as if they were unsure of what to do. As Randall had stated, these were not professional soldiers, just ordinary men drafted in by a lunatic. This was another thing in our favour.

The others began to respond to the action. Prisoners leapt to their feet all around, closing in on the guards. I was hidden in the chaos; the guards had no idea from which direction the original missiles had been thrown. Someone else had also taken up arms, and the guards were suddenly showered with rocks and stones and handfuls of dust… anything that could be used to distract them. None of this caused them any real damage, but it gave us enough time to rush them and make things difficult.

It took the guards a few moments to settle themselves enough to open fire.

Gunshots tore the air; bodies fell; blood flew like black water in the early morning dimness.

I heard the sounds of commotion from the pit, and was thrilled to see three figures scurrying insect-like up the sides and over the lip. Moving quickly, they converged on the guards from behind, overpowering them while they were occupied by our diversion and pressing them to the ground. Other figures soon followed suit. The remaining gunshots grew muffled; somebody cried out. Then I heard a dreadful rending sound, as if the guards were being torn apart.

Literally torn apart...

That was when I remembered the other guard – the one left at the gate, ready to clock off and get some rest. I glanced in that direction, and saw him running for the house. He was crying out, but I could not understand his words. I hesitated for a second to scoop up another fist-sized stone and then followed him, desperation lending me speed that I did not normally possess. I gained on him quickly, and suddenly realised that I was yelling. It was a war cry, a howl of attack. I had become a warrior.

I threw the stone as I ran, and my aim was perfect. This was the kind of thing that only ever happened in dreams, or in the movies, but it was real, it was happening to me here and now, and it was nothing short of empowering. The rock hit the back of his head, sending him crashing forward, and then down. He fell on his face. I kept running. When I reached him he was scrabbling around in search of his dropped weapon, so I kicked him in the side of the face. I heard the loud cracking of bone. Then, calmly, I picked up his rifle and pointed it at him.

Voices were carried from the direction of the house. Lights came on. I pulled the trigger and watched as the guard's head split down one side, turning the ground red. His ruined head dropped abruptly, the forehead hitting the ground with a nauseating wet thud.

Heading towards the rear of the house, I caught sight of Randall. His face was white, powdered with quicklime: he looked like a stylised Japanese demon. He was raising a rifle in the air, and howling like a wolf. As I ran past, Randall led a group of people out of the Gulag gate and towards the guards who were even now approaching. I heard gunfire; the air was filled with screams. This was my chance.

Leaving them to their battle, I ran towards mine. Manisa and Becky needed me, and there was no way that I would let them down. I had failed too many people already, and now was the time to change things. These women, my group, would not die here: we would walk away from this together, or not at all. It did not occur to me at the time that all thoughts of my wife had deserted me; only afterwards did I experience the intense guilt of forgetting her, of putting her last.

The back of the house was in darkness. No lights shone at the windows, and heavy wooden shutters had been pulled down and secured over the glass. I spotted the timber hatch Randall had mentioned immediately. It was locked and bolted. I was overcome with a deadening sense of defeat until I recalled the rifle in my hand. I had no practical experience with firearms, but in my murderous state I had somehow managed to shoot a man and kill him. I looked at the gun, but it was alien to me, something I only barely understood.

I pointed the rifle at the lock, turned my head to the side in case of shrapnel, and pulled the trigger. Once again, the rifle responded to my touch, but this time I missed my target. It took three more shots until I hit the lock, and it shattered as if made out of plastic. I pulled the trigger again, just to be sure or because I'd already gone over the edge, but nothing happened. Either the bullets had run out or there was something I needed to do with the mechanism to make it work again. I stared at the rifle, blinking. Hit it with the palm of my hand. Then I threw it to the ground, realising that it had it had served its purpose and was no longer of any use to me.

This had all happened so quickly. Everything was moving too fast. I paused and took a deep breath, then another, trying to slow down the action. My vision dimmed, then brightened; I saw a shimmering pattern of light. I closed my eyes and waited, and then when I opened them again the world seemed to pulse gently, as if I were glimpsing the heartbeat of the planet. The rhythm was stilted, damaged; but the heart still beat. It still worked.

I bent to the hatch and grabbed the metal handle, pulling at it with every bit of strength I could muster. The gunfire behind me had petered out; either the battle was in the process of being won, or almost everyone was dead and both sides had lost. I did not divert my attention away from the hatch to find out. There was no time; I needed to keep moving forward, towards the object of my desire.

My desire? Is that what motivated me then, what drove me onward?

Even now, I cannot be sure.

No matter how hard I pulled on the hatch, it would not budge. The wood was stuck in its frame, and I began to realise that all my good intentions might come to nought. Emptiness rose within me; it threatened to engulf me from the inside out.

"Hey!"

I turned around, my arms hanging limp at my sides. It was over. I was done.

"Need some help?" Randall's dusty face grinned at me in the gloom. He took several steps forward, still gripping the rifle he had liberated from a militia guard. "That looks like a two-man job to me."

"Thanks." A single gunshot sounded from the other side of the house. "Did we win?"

Randall's smile dropped. He shook his head. "We beat the guards, but the noise drew the leftovers from the woods. They're storming the fence. I'm not sure how long it'll hold."

Together we tugged at the hatch, and I was relieved when it opened. The hinges creaked; there was the sound of splitting timber. We threw back the double doors and peered down into darkness. A set of steps led down into the basement area, and there was no light down there.

"You first," said Randall. His eyes blazed through the layer of quicklime. As I looked closer, I picked out evidence of burning on his flesh.

I nodded. Then, bracing myself, I stepped down into the dark.

Randall followed close behind, and closed the hatch after us. Just before complete blackness took my vision, I glimpsed a flashlight on a narrow Formica shelf screwed to the wall by my head. I reached out and grabbed the torch, flicking it on. The beam cut a line through the darkness, but on either side of the wavering yellow light I could see nothing.

"Let's make this quick," said Randall, at my back. "I don't know how long we can hold off those leftovers. There aren't many, but even in small numbers they can cause a lot of problems. I don't want to go back up there and find everyone dead." He laughed; the same hideous laugh as I'd heard before, in the Gulag. I realised that it was a psychological tick: a sign that he was reaching his breaking point, or perhaps a pressure valve.

"Come on," I whispered. "Let's get the women out."

We moved forward, into the blackness, and I felt the walls closing in on me. The basement smelled of moist earth, and it was unbelievably hot down there. The walls, I realised as I stuck out a hand, were lined with timber, not properly caulked. When it rained heavily, the atmosphere would become humid and uncomfortable.

We were in a narrow entrance corridor, and as it opened out into a room I began to make out more details. The basement was not a large space, but it had been utilised for storage. There were old bicycles down there, a rusty fridge-freezer sat on a raised plinth (possibly as a precaution against flooding), and a whole lot of other defunct domestic apparatus was littered here and there throughout the musty area.

Up ahead, along a second tight channel, another room seemed to emanate a gentle glow. There was a light on through there, but it was soft and not very powerful. As we passed through this second area, I realised that there was a single bare bulb hanging from the ceiling. The cable ran across the clad ceiling, down the timbered wall, and into a socket set a foot above the floor. More wooden plinths ran around the room's perimeter, and most of them were filled with stacks of torn papers and water-swollen books. Somewhere a generator hummed. A steel filing cabinet stood in one corner, its drawers containing shredded paperwork. Wire cages lined the left hand wall.

Cages.

I stopped and stared. The women were silent, drawn close together for comfort. They stared at me through the heavy wire mesh.

"Shit," said Randall. Faces turned towards us. Someone whimpered like a dog.

I could not make out any individuals among the small group of women, but I hoped that Manisa and Becky where there.

"Mack?" There she was; I would recognise her voice anywhere.

"Yes. Are you two okay?"

"Get out. Quick." This was Becky. The whimpering sound came again, as if punctuating her words.

"I'm afraid that's too late." The voice – this one belonging to a man – came from behind me.

I turned, shoulders slumped. Thwaite was standing in the opening through which we'd just entered, a small silver handgun pointed at us. "I just want my friends. Let me take them, and you'll never see us again." Desperation cracked my voice.

Thwaite smiled. He was wearing a dusty black bowler hat, a skin-tight leather tank top and a pair of garish Bermuda shorts. On his feet was a pair of snakeskin cowboy boots. In any other situation, I might have laughed. But in the context of the moment, his outfit was more horrifying than it was comical, and spoke volumes about the man's state of mind. It was as if each of his increasingly bizarre outfits reflected a separate aspect of himself, like different skins worn during the stages of a transformation.

"Come on, Thwaite. You don't need us." I spread my hands in a gesture of defeat.

"I don't *need* anyone. I have, however, discovered that I enjoy collecting slaves and breeders. It's good for me – keeps me from losing my mind completely." He waved the gun barrel in front of him, making a tight little circle in the air.

Randall took a step forward, opened his mouth, and for a moment I was confused to see his teeth shatter and speckle the air like small white insects. The gunshot seemed to enter the cramped space a split second after the damage was done, and only then did I realise that Thwaite had shot Randall in the face.

The women screamed.

Randall slumped to the ground.

"I didn't like that twat," said Thwaite, stepping fully into the room. "He was a trouble-maker. Good worker, though, which is why we let him live and didn't put him in the pit with the others." The heels of his cowboy boots scraped on the floor as he walked towards me. He was even swaggering, like a poor man's John Wayne.

"They were all alive when you got here? You killed them?"

He shook his head. The bowler slipped slightly, but did not fall. "We cleansed the building, that's all. Put a few pests to sleep." He took another step towards me.

I looked around me, noticing for the first time the other paraphernalia in the room. There was a surprisingly small, narrow medical table, a piece of kit with rubber tubes and dials. A stack of medical books with animals on the covers. "You're not a doctor, are you?"

Thwaite giggled. "I was a veterinary surgeon, actually. I used to care for the security dogs they kept here – those awful mutts. I put them to sleep, too, when I took over. They were a symbol of the past, you see."

He was waving the gun again; I guessed that it was a giveaway of his intention to use it, like the telltale twitch of a lover's penis before he ejaculates. Because that's exactly what was going on here: Thwaite was getting off, enjoying a sexual kick from the threat of killing. I could see it in the tent of his stupid Bermuda shorts, and the way he was growing short of breath. In the shine of his red cheeks beneath the brim of the silly costume bowler hat.

He was now close enough to touch. I knew I had one chance, and if I failed we were all dead.

I moved as quick as I could, leaping forward and grabbing at the gun with one hand, in the hope that if he fired the weapon the bullet might go wide. With my other hand I took a swipe at his head – it wasn't even a proper punch, just a fist flailing in the general direction of his face.

Thwaite's head whipped backwards, more to try and dodge the blow than because of the impact. He staggered a few steps, the gun falling from his grasp, and as he backed away down the corridor I followed him, capitalising on his panicked retreat. I spotted the gun and picked it up on my way past, my finger sliding clumsily over the trigger.

Thwaite began to run, heading for the hatch – which was now open; I could just about make out the brightening sky through the open square. "No!" he yelled, glancing back at me over one shoulder. His boot heels scuffed the ground; his baggy shorts flapped against his skinny thighs; the bowler hat fell from his head and rolled away into an unseen corner. I had to be hard. Tough. Just like when I was young, and Kay needed protecting.

I shot him once in the small of the back. I was aiming for his head but was happy enough to hit him anywhere. The leather tank top darkened a few inches above his backside, and his knees buckled, sending him crashing down. He tried to continue towards the exit, crawling and using his hands to drag himself through the dirt. Then, after several seconds of clumsy scrabbling motions, he gave up and lay still. A weird croaking sound came from his throat, and he pressed his cheek to the ground. His eyes were open. He did not blink.

I turned away from the absurd dying figure of Dr. Thwaite and returned to the cages, where I could release the women he had so charmingly christened breeders. They had fallen silent, as if in amazement at the ease with which I had despatched their captor.

I smiled, coldly. Then I went to Manisa. I could only hope that she still recognised me now that I had become a cold-blooded killer.

THREE:
THE LAST WAVE

They swarmed out of the woods, sniffing the air like animals. She was in a cluster near the front, her arms pumping wildly and her short legs working hard to carry her towards the fence line. There were strange constructions there, with others like her pinned to them. Their eyes were open but they could not see; some of their mouths were filled with dark-coloured petals. The song of static had ceased to pour from them. They had gone on to the next place, where everything was better.

She increased her pace, not knowing why. She felt nothing but the urge to destroy, and all that kept her from picking up a stick and slamming the sharp end into her own eye, her brain, was the fact that she had cut herself. She touched her body as she ran, fingering the winding loops which hung from her belly. They were soft and wet; she wrapped them around her hands and wrists, like bracelets. Tugged. Static flared behind her teeth and she opened her mouth to sing.

She could not speak, yet she managed to communicate with the others around her. They had all known each other, long ago, before the change had come upon them. She knew their faces, but not what those faces meant to her. They were just vaguely familiar arrangements of eyes and noses and mouths.

She ran on. They all did. Towards the fence.

Raising her hands, she opened her mouth and hissed. The static inside her was released into the open air, sending a signal to those who ran with her. They all took up the call. They sang together.

It was the music of mass destruction, a tune they were all beginning to know well.

The people behind the fence pointed things at them, and there came loud noises. Some of her fellows tumbled to the earth, and some of them got back up. Pieces flew from their bodies, but the sensation was good; it stopped the urge from overtaking them.

She watched in silence as her upraised left hand vaporised. Then, as another pellet made contact with her shoulder, she stumbled.

The fence was drawing near. Not long now… a few more paces and she would be there. She looked around and hissed louder, signalling the ones who ran at her side. Their beautiful black eyes burned in the night. The sound of their voice – the communal song – was blissful.

Then, as she hit the fence, something spilled from her. Whatever was inside her belly came out, spooling into the dirt. She glanced down and watched; it was a strange sight, and brought back odd memories: thoughts of playing and sitting at a small desk writing her name.

A word came to her, then – no, it was a name. Her name. But as soon as meaning came it flew out of reach, as if borne on wings like a bird. Birds. They flew in the sky, didn't they? Facts were returning to her; things were coming back. The tension at the base of her skull had slackened, allowing inside pictures of the things she had once known. She missed none of them. Not one thing. They were dead, just pictures, and they could not touch her.

She climbed the fence, reaching out for someone... clawing at a face that looked as if it might have once smiled and laughed and even wept. She tore, pulling away the flesh like a mask, and then scrambled wildly over the lovely sharpness at the top of the fence. She felt herself slicing. This was good. It kept the urge to end her existence behind her — she was still outrunning that urge, even now. She had to keep ahead, if only until she could end another black spark along with her own.

Just as she tumbled over and rolled on the ground, she felt something tugging. Her head was pushed to the side, and suddenly her vision on one side was erased. She could barely see a thing, but she saw enough to grab one of the people nearby and sink her hands into the soft matter of his belly, where the warm stuff was kept.

She pushed her fingers, pushed what was left of her mind. Then, just as lightning flared somewhere and the song of static came to an end, she realised that she had been lied to. There was no place better than this. She didn't want to go. She wanted... wanted... she just wanted, and that was all.

She wanted more than this.

CHAPTER 24

The concept of time had become irrelevant.

I have no idea how long it took me to open the cages which stretched the length of the basement wall, but I found a big set of keys hanging from a nail and set to work as quickly and quietly as I could to find the right ones. I could hear no sounds from above ground; the fear that everyone up there had been killed goaded me on. Randall had told me that leftovers had breached the wire, and since then everything had become confusing.

Something in my bones told me that my worst fears were simply an intuition of what had really happened: the only things moving up there were already dead, and barely human. I could only guess at how many there were.

The fact that I had just killed two men in cold blood seemed strangely distant from my thoughts, as if it could no longer touch me. I knew what I'd done was wrong – or would have been, in another world, a world that we had now left behind. But necessity is the mother of invention, and it seemed that I had invented a way to kill without feeling even the slightest pang of remorse. I had successfully compartmentalised the act, shutting it off in a small room in my mind. Just as I always did with all distasteful events.

I knew that I would pay for this later, that there would be a psychological debt which would be called in at some unspecified point in my life, but for now I felt able to deal with the murders. I was dealing with everything else, so why not this?

Finally I opened the cage doors, and women streamed past me, some of them touching me in silent thanks and others simply running blind. Some of them were half naked. Even the ones fully clothed looked frightened and worn out, and their faces were etched with an emotion I could not identify.

"Are you okay?" Manisa fell into my arms, but not in a swooning maiden-in-distress kind of way, she simply grabbed hold of me to prove that I was real and not some kind of delusion brought on by the effects of terror.

"Yeah." The most frightening thing about this situation was that I actually *was* okay. Thwaite's blood was not upon me; his filth had not touched me. I felt no different than before I had killed him. I was the same man, a man in control.

"Let's get the fuck out of here." Becky was standing by Thwaite's corpse. She had picked up the gun and held it as if she knew what she was doing. As I watched, she did something to the weapon and pulled out the ammunition clip. Becky inspected the ammo, nodded, and then slid the clip back into the handle. "We're good," she said. "Almost fully loaded."

I stared at her, wondering where she had learned to handle firearms.

"There's a lot you don't know about me," she said, trying to smile. Her lips wriggled across her bared teeth, but the smile was only half formed and rather scary.

The other women had already fled past us and out into the night, through the open entrance hatch. I glanced at the hatch, gripping Manisa's arm, and then took a step towards Becky. "Lead on, then," I said, nodding.

Becky approached the hatch with the gun held up at shoulder level, ready for action. She looked like an insane TV cop. Her arms were bare; either she or someone else had taken off her shirt and she was standing like some crazed vision in her bra and trousers. There were old scars along her forearms; lines of hard, white tissue that drew the eye.

Manisa was still fully clothed, and I wondered if Becky had been molested or simply partially stripped to calm her down – she was an aggressive woman, and I doubted that Thwaite's men would have been able to handle her without establishing some kind of physical dominance. The threat of rape seemed the kind of psychological weapon these people might use. Particularly since rape was exactly what they had in mind. It was obvious that some of the other captive women had already been subjected to the attentions of Thwaite's studs; I only hoped that I had been in time to spare my two friends such horror.

I glanced at Thwaite's body as we passed by, and felt the urge to spit on him. "Did they hurt you?" I turned to Manisa, staring into her big dark eyes.

"She took the brunt of it." She indicated Becky with a slight shake of her head. "She fought like a mad woman and they pinned her down and took off her shirt. They grabbed her breasts and told her they'd cut them off and use them as tobacco pouches if she didn't calm down."

Her face was pale, the natural colour barely there at all. Yet still she was beautiful.

I watched Becky's back as she pulled herself up to the hatch and poked her head above the ground. She was taut and well-muscled, which was something I'd previously attributed to a tough gym regime. But now that I had seen her with the gun, and heard how she'd acted to divert the attention of Thwaite's militia, I began to reassess my feelings towards this strange, agile young woman. There was more to Becky than I had ever suspected – perhaps more than even Mitch had been aware of. I realised that he'd never told me about what she did with her time outside the office, and if I was being honest I doubted that he had ever even asked her. Mitch, despite being my only friend, had been a selfish bastard. I could admit that now, after everything we had been through; and the honesty of my thoughts felt like a spiritual cleansing.

"I can see movement round the side of the house." Becky's voice was cold, hard. During the time she had spent in the cage with the other women, something about her had changed. We were all changing, all the time; this was just another facet of that change. "If we can slip around the other way, we might be able to get to the front without being seen. We left the keys in Bob's car – I remember that. Let's hope nobody has taken them." She turned to face us, and I barely even recognised her. Her eyes were sunken; her cheeks were cleaved to her bones.

In that moment I knew that Becky had both assimilated and dealt with the facts of Mitch's death. That part of her life was over, and I doubted that she would ever even mention his name again. What else was she hiding, this woman? What other secrets had been swallowed and digested and retained deep within her surprisingly tough frame?

"Shit!" She turned to us again. "Big trouble."

"What is it?" Manisa remained at my side, her thigh pressed against me. She was warm and shaking, her leg was tensed. I imagined that I could feel her heart beating through her skin and clothes.

"There are too many of them out there. Leftovers. I think they've broken down the fence and taken over the compound. That's why there's no more gunfire. They've probably killed everyone… and I'd assume that a lot of them have gone down in the process. The rest are scouring for survivors." She climbed back down the steps, pulling the twin doors of the hatch closed as she went. Darkness engulfed us, but I could still hear her voice. "We're going to have to make our way through the house."

There was a scarred and battered wooden door at the far end of the room which contained the cages. The door was closed, but if it were locked we already had a set of keys. I left Manisa's side and walked towards the door, fumbling with the keys. After a few panicked seconds, I managed to locate the right one and unlock the door. When I opened it the house's interior came into view; a few concrete steps led up on the other side, and beyond them I could make out the white goods and work surfaces of a large kitchen.

"Can you hear anyone moving around up there?" Becky stood at my side, the firearm raised. I glanced at her, and then looked back up the steps into the kitchen. All was silent up there; there were no signs of life. But life was not what I was listening for. I was trying to pinpoint evidence of something which no longer lived, a life form completely different from the rest of us. Something *leftover*...

"Just keep that gun at the ready. You clearly know how to use it, so don't hesitate if anything jumps out." I took a step up, trusting the women to follow close behind. Then another. Another. When finally I reached the top of the steps, I eased away from the entrance and waited for Becky, and then Manisa, to come through.

It was dim in the kitchen, but I could still make out the details around me. The first thing I noticed was a knife rack. It was filled with professional-level cutting tools, so I walked over and selected a large cleaver. I hefted the cleaver in my hand, testing its weight, and decided that it felt right. If anyone approached me, this would do the trick.

"I'll go first," I said, making my way across the room to the doorway. The door was half open; weak light spilled through the gap. I paused when I reached it, and peered through. Holding my breath in case there was anyone out there, I stared along a short corridor. On the right was a set of stairs leading up to the next floor – perhaps a staff access. At the other end of the short hallway there was yet another door, which I assumed would take us towards the front of the house and the main exit. The car was parked a few hundred yards from the conservatory – if we ran we might make it, as long as our luck held.

"Come on. Get a move on." Manisa was pushing us from behind. I could understand her eagerness to get out of the place, but did not like the idea of taking any more unnecessary risks.

"Shush. Just let me make sure it's okay first." Timbers creaked, but I could not be sure if it was the sound of someone moving about upstairs or simply the building settling. I waited, but the sound did not come again. "Okay. Let's move. Stick close and if anything happens just run for the fucking door." As plans went it was pretty weak – but there was no time to formulate any further course of action. We had to move, and we had to move now.

One by one, we trotted out of the kitchen and along the hallway. I glanced up the stairs, but only weak daylight caught my eye. Pushing open the door, I peered out at what I recognised as the main reception area. The front door beckoned, but I was too cautious to make a mad dash for the exit.

"What's wrong?" Becky prodded my side.

"Just wait... I want to be sure." We all paused, holding our breath, and when no sounds came I decided to move. "Quickly. Out the door, straight down the drive, and into the car." I went first, checking the area, gripping the cleaver. Becky came second, the gun held steady in both of her hands. Manisa followed. Her thin face was stricken by what could only be repressed panic.

Again there was a staircase to our right, but this time it was the main route to the upper floors. We had used those stairs before, going up to our rooms, which now felt like years ago. I looked up, but again saw no evidence of movement. "Come on, now. Let's get out." I let the women overtake me, while I kept my gaze focused on the stairs. It was stupid, really, because the most dangerous point in our vicinity was obviously the doors to my left – and that's precisely where trouble emerged from.

"Don't move."

I turned to face the owner of the voice, and was once again confronted by the sight of Thwaite's man Tallow, with his wispy hair and his angry face. "Don't shoot." The words were reflexive; they came out unbidden when I saw the rifle in his hand. Tallow looked agitated; his white boiler suit was spattered with blood. He swayed in the doorway as if he were drunk.

"They're everywhere... killing us all, killing themselves. Killing everyone. Kids. Just kids." His voice was poised on the edge of hysteria. He had clearly been confronted by a situation that his own violence could not resolve – indeed, a greater violence than any he could offer had reared up before him. "They're... everywhere." His eyes became unfocused, and he lowered the rifle. "Fucking children."

Becky chose that moment to act. "Put it down," she yelled, firmly. "Get away from the weapon and walk away." The way she spoke, the firmness in her voice; it made me suspect that she perhaps worked as a special constable or was a member of the Territorial Army in her spare time. Again I realised how little I actually knew about this woman – and the origins of her courage.

Amazingly, Tallow did exactly as he was requested. As I watched, he raised his empty hands and backed away, retreating into the main room, where Thwaite had arrogantly taken audience with us when we had first arrived and invaded his unstable little community. He rocked on his heels, and for a moment I thought he might drop to the floor.

Becky moved forward and bent at the knees, keeping the handgun trained on Tallow's retreating figure. She picked up the rifle in her free hand. "Here. Just point the fucker and pull the trigger." She passed me the handgun and cradled the rifle in her arms, like a newborn baby. Her finger curled instinctively around the trigger. The tenderness she showed the weapon was almost nauseating.

I glanced through the doorway, into the main room, and saw Tallow sitting on the floor with his legs spread wide apart. He was staring down between his knees, at the polished floor, and mumbling to himself. There was so much red: blood on his boiler suit, blood in his wispy hair. But nothing of any importance showed behind his eyes.

Tallow no longer represented a threat, so I turned away from him and headed towards the front door. Pushing it open, I stepped out into the conservatory. The first thing I saw was broken glass – most of the panes had been shattered, and a body hung across jagged teeth of glass, almost cut in half at the waist.

There was a young girl standing about ten feet in front of me. She was staring right at me, her large black eyes fixed on my face. She was covered in blood.

"Oh, shit." Manisa was once again by my side. She gripped my hand, her fingers curling around the gun I was holding so uselessly. In the other hand, I squeezed the handle of the cleaver. I knew that I would be unable to use either weapon on the grubby creature which stood before us. "It's a child."

I watched the girl. She must have been around nine or ten when she became a leftover. She was wearing a purple school blazer over a torn white shirt, and her bloodied legs stuck out beneath a shredded purple pleated skirt. There was a lot of blood on her exposed midriff, and when I looked closer I saw that her innards were hanging from an open wound. One of her hands was missing at the wrist. Something glistened in the other hand, and as she raised it I saw that she was gripping a length of her own intestine. The other end was still attached to the wound in her side; it slithered like a snake when she moved.

"Don't move," I said, not knowing what to do.

The girl opened her mouth and the now familiar hiss of static erupted from her throat. Her black eyes bulged; they looked as if they might burst from her head. Then, as if a subtle shift in my perception had occurred, I heard what she was saying.

The horrible static hiss was actually a voice – no, it was many voices. And they were all repeating the same message: *They did it. You did it. End it now.*

I stared at the leftover, the girl, the nightmare. I stared at her and I listened. The sound issuing from her mouth was made up of millions of voices, all screaming across a distance so great that I doubted there were units in existence to measure it. Those voices, they came from another place, another world...perhaps even another dimension. I listened to the sound; the grating voice of countless lost souls crying out for connection, reaching desperately for communion. Their message was *our* message: it was the end.

The end.

It was the end of it all.

"Step out of the way." Becky pushed past us, the rifle held at her shoulder. She marched forward, her steps slow and purposeful. For a moment I thought she might keep on going, walking right through the girl, but after a few steps she halted, her shoulders tensed.

I waited. The girl hissed again. The sound was rasping, metallic. The voices grew louder. Did Becky hear them, or Manisa? Or was this all simply a product of my own guilt and remorse?

They did it. You did it. End it now.

Becky pulled the trigger. She did it early, possibly before she had a chance to think about what she was doing, who she was shooting, and I had no time to turn away before the little girl's head burst like a popped balloon. Blood and bone and gristle flew everywhere; a shower of red and white and black.

Black.

Her brains... the pieces that flew from her shattered skull were black. Just like her eyes. Thick black matter, like pulped liquorice, spattered her shoulders and speckled Becky's vacant face. So much black stuff on her white skin, sullying it...

I acted quickly, realising that we had to move. I tried not to think about the voices. We had to get out of there. I rushed at Becky, knocking down the gun and grabbing her arm. "Go, go..." I dragged her then, pulling her towards the busted down door, and we made our way along the driveway towards where the vehicles were parked. Small figures darted here and there, other school kids pursuing their own destruction. I guessed that there must be some kind of boarding school nearby and that everyone there had succumbed to what Thwaite had christened the Kamikaze Syndrome.

There were bodies everywhere – dead militia, dead prisoners, self-vanquished leftovers.

Thank God the keys were still in Bob's car, right where he'd left them. I jumped in the front and the women climbed in the back, Becky pointing the rifle out of the rear window and taking pot shots at the stunted figures which capered in the darkness. Then, before we had a chance to react, the back door was flung open and hands were grabbing at Becky. Manisa kicked out, while at the same time she tried to grab Becky's hair.

But she was dragged out of the car, her arms and legs flailing. She did not even scream. The small figure who held her wrested the rifle from her grasp, then pushed her to the ground. I saw the white arc of teeth as it grinned, then I saw it raise the rifle and bring it down repeatedly on Becky's body, her head...and at the last, at the very last second, it turned back towards us.

"Drive! Drive now, Mack!" Manisa was at breaking point. Now that we were in the car, she was allowing herself the room to snap. "Just fucking go!" We both knew that Becky was dead, so the only option was to do as Manisa said and get the hell out of there.

I went. I fucking went. The wheels spun on loose dirt as I jammed my foot down onto the accelerator, and the car lurched forward, its rear end skidding in a wide arc. The small figure – I think it was a boy, a thin boy in school blazer and shorts – ran at us from an angle, and then threw itself beneath the rear wheels as I slammed the car into second gear. I felt the tyres churning his tiny body, reducing it to road kill, and then we slammed over the corpse.

I fought against the cold, hard urge to reverse over him and make sure the job was done. I tried to remind myself that he had once been a child, and that he had not asked to be left over... none of them had asked for that.

Then we were away, barrelling down the drive and out through the open gate, onto the dirt track and heading in the direction of the main road. We had started out as four, and now our number was halved, cut in two as if by a blade.

We were out. We had escaped. But at what cost? What price had we paid for our freedom, and how long could it possibly last?

CHAPTER 25

The next half-hour is fractured, incomplete, like the remnants of a dream I might once have had; a mesh of random half-glimpsed images and the terrible sense of being pursued. The landscape passed by in a haze of dull brown and black shadow, and I was barely even aware of Manisa as she wept into her fist in the back seat. I only stopped the car when I was sure that there was nobody following us — this time I checked, just to be sure.

I stared at the road ahead, wondering if there was anything good waiting for me up there.

I got out of the car and stood at the side of the road, in a narrow lay-by. Daylight flared in my vision. I took out my mobile phone and stared at it. It was dead, just like my heart. Feeling sad, I put it back in my pocket. Just as I moved my hand away, the phone began to vibrate.

I did not want to take the phone back out of my pocket, but what choice did I have? I knew that I would see another message, and that it would be more of the same, but there was no way that I could ignore the phone.

I took the mobile out of my pocket and lifted it to my face, to my eyes.

The screen was lit up. There were words glowing on it, as if they had been summoned from the ether, or perhaps even from the depths of my own slowly breaking mind.

YOU DID IT

The words changed, morphed, bleeding away and then back again, but different this time.

END IT

I felt tears on my cheeks but for some reason did not connect them with the act of crying. It felt like rain soaking my face.

END IT ALL

Again the words danced and changed and revealed another line of the continuous message.

END IT ALL NOW

I almost responded to the imperative; I nearly did what I was being told to do. The gun was lost somewhere – probably dropped in our haste to escape – but I still had the cleaver; it was back in the car, lying on the front passenger seat. If it had been in my hand I would have used it. On myself. I know I would.

Those crackling voices... the voices inside the girl... had they been speaking only to me or to us all – every single survivor left on the face of the earth?

They did it. You did it. End it now.

The message was clear; all that remained uncertain was who it was meant for, and where it had come from. Deep inside me, I was certain that we would never truly know.

I threw the phone away, hurling it as hard and as far as I could across the rough landscape. I heard the handset break against a rock or a patch of solid ground. The sound was not a comfort. There was too much of an echo of that awful static scream, the one I'd heard from the little girl and from the others – the unseen mouths of so many others. I thought of black eyes and open mouths, of creatures whose one aim was to end it all. End it all now.

You did it.

The phone began to ring. I glanced over at the car, where Manisa was now leaning out of the door and gulping down air. Her face was stretched, as if someone had pummelled it. She looked at me, and then in the direction of the phone. Then she began to dry-heave.

End it now.

I walked over to her, placed a hand on her shoulder. "What are we going to do?" I was no hero, and my pathetic attempts at control had ended in the deaths of Bob and Becky. I was not fit to be in charge of a house pet, let alone to lead a group of people through this nightmare landscape. I was a joke, a failure. A man who heard voices where perhaps there were none.

"Let's just drive. Get to my parents' place." Manisa sat up straight, got out of the car, and hugged me. She smelled warm and wet, like the promise of a storm. Her breath tickled the side of my neck. I ran my hands across her back, down to her backside, and cupped her buttocks. Kay's face hovered in my vision, smiling, forgiving me my trespasses...

I pulled away from Manisa, and lurched back into the car, my chest tight and my eyes burning. Manisa climbed in next to me, strapped herself in, and stared through the windscreen. Despite the cold wash of daylight the road ahead was dark – it had always been dark, for as long as I could remember. I could no longer recall the light. There was no real illumination left in the world, not for the likes of us.

Dark, the whole world; all of it, so very fucking dark.

We drove on, heading deep into that ragged terrain, ploughing further into a broken land, a suicide country: a place of severed roads and empty vessels. Behind us, the sun was shimmering like an unstable nova, but a metaphorical night still gripped the world. We did not speak. There was little left to be said.

CHAPTER 26

When we reached the outskirts of Bourneville we were so very tired. Frost glittered on the pavements and the streets we drove along were all quiet and empty, as if the entire population of this affluent suburb were merely sleeping.

I could smell chocolate in the air from the nearby factory, as if the odour was a permanent part of the place. The aroma was strangely pleasant, and I notched down the window an inch to better take it in.

The first body we saw hanging from a telephone wire negated the illusion of calm. It was an old man, and the laces of several pairs of running shoes were wrapped tightly around his neck; the shoes had been thrown so that they spun around the wire, locking them in place. I had no idea how he had even got up there, or if he had killed himself or been done away with by a surprisingly nimble leftover. His eyes were closed. I could not make out if they were black.

As we turned a corner we saw the rest of the bodies, and Manisa buried her face in my shoulder. There were scores of them, lying on the ground, hanging from lampposts, smouldering in the remnants of bushes gone to charcoal.

The whole suburb seemed dead. Every resident had either become a leftover or been despatched by the resulting murderous horde.

"I can't..." Manisa still hid her face. "I can't look at them."

The car coasted towards the kerb, and I was careful not to hit any of the bodies lying there, in the road and across the footpath, their head or feet or arms in the gutter. The whole place was dead: dead people, dead houses, dead air. Nothing moved. Nothing lived. It was a suicide town.

"Which house belongs to your parents?" I eased Manisa away from me, making a gap between us. Despite everything that was going on, and the vicinity of so much death, I still felt the ghost of arousal. Even here, even now, I wanted her.

"It's just along there... number seventeen." She pointed ahead, her hand shaking. She was trying to keep her eyes off the carnage, but it was impossible to ignore. "Will you come with me?"

"Of course I will. But we'll have to leave the car here. There are too many bodies in the way to drive up to the door." This whole conversation was surreal, and that was the only reason I could keep it up. If things had been more real and less insane, I could not have retained a sense of composure.

Manisa nodded. Her head rubbed against my chest.

"Are you sure you want to do this? If you like, you can stay in the car and I'll check the house. If there's anyone there I'll find them."

She moved her head and looked up at me. Her eyes were moist and filled with emotion. It hurt to see her that way, and I felt the urge to smother her and hide her from this horror. "I have to see for myself."

"I understand." And I did; of course I did.

We left the car parked at the kerb and began to walk along the pretty little street. Well-maintained gardens had become grave plots. The clean streets were now littered with the dead. Broken windows, shattered doors, cars and vans driven into walls. Chaos had reigned here for a short time, and by the look of some of the human remains it had all been a part of the initial wave of the suicide plague. Flesh was beginning to rot, even in the cold air, and blood had dried to dark stains on the paths and walkways.

We reached the door of number seventeen, and Manisa paused for a moment at the front gate. She reached out her hand and touched the gate, lightly, as if it were hot, and then snatched her hand back and held it against her stomach.

I gave her some time. Waiting, just waiting. There was no rush, not now, so near the end of this; everything had its own pace, and I was reluctant to hurry my silent companion. Then, as if she had made a decision, Manisa pushed open the gate. It squeaked only quietly as it swung on the hinges. We made our way along the drive, passing what I assumed was Manisa's parents' car – a two-year-old Ford Focus, black paintwork dusty in the early sunlight. Light frost twinkled on the windscreen.

The front door was open. Just a crack, but enough to be a giveaway. I knew they were dead; Manisa knew this, too, but she struggled to maintain the illusion that all might be well. She pushed the door wide and stepped through, faltering for just a second. If I had not noticed the slight stumble as she crossed the threshold, I might have thought that she was handling this incredibly well.

"You okay? You don't have to do this."

She turned to me, eyes flashing, and for a moment she looked like someone else, a different person from the one I had come to know... and, yes, to love, in a way. "I *do* have to do this. Don't you even think of telling me that I don't."

I backed away from her, just a half a step, but room enough to give her the space to work this out. Then, after another few seconds, she touched my arm and let out a breath. "Stay with me."

We walked along the hallway and into the living room. There was nobody there. The room was a mess, but there were no signs of anyone still being around. The television screen had been shattered, so thankfully there could be no message beamed through it, and the shelves had been pulled from the walls.

"Oh, God. Stay with me, Mack..."

I followed Manisa back out of the room and up the stairs – she angled her body so that I could not pass her and take the lead. She wanted to confront whatever was here before I did, and I could respect her decision to do so. This was her home, these were her family – whatever might be left of them.

There was a mess at the top of the stairs. Clothes and papers and books, all scattered across the landing. A body lay amid the mess, face-up and staring at the ceiling. It was a woman, and her eyes were open: they were jet black, like painted studs in a doll's face. The bloodied handle of a carving knife was sticking out of the side of her neck.

Manisa stepped calmly over the corpse. Her entire attitude had altered, her posture becoming more intent. She was bracing herself, preparing for what we both expected to see.

The master bedroom had been trashed. A big fight had occurred here. The two people had obviously put up a lot of resistance. The body of a large man dressed in pyjamas was sprawled on the bed. His torso had been split and opened from throat to crotch, and his insides were out, smeared across the duvet. On the floor at his feet was a thin woman. She was naked. One arm had been wrenched from its socket – and I say wrenched, because it clearly had been: the meat of the socket was twisted and bruised rather than sliced.

Manisa stared at her parents. She did not cry. She just looked at them, her hands shifting into an attitude of prayer, cupped beneath her pained face. She said nothing. Just stood there, staring and shaking and wrestling with her emotions.

I stepped backwards, softly, gently, not wanting to disturb her yet scared to leave her completely. I stood against the bedroom wall, waiting for her to finish.

I knew that I should be thinking of Kay and the baby, but all of my thoughts were with Manisa. It was like a stepping-off point, a moment of utter clarity and acceptance...and yet, still I was unable to face the truth. I had to continue my journey, if only for the sake of closing the circle.

"I'm done." Manisa's voice was a lot steadier than I would have expected. "I'm finished here. Let's go." When she turned around her features looked hard and empty. Something inside her had snapped, and I had not even heard it break. She walked across the room, right into my arms, but I could not move. I clenched my fists at my sides, unable to raise my hands to embrace her. "Hold me," she said. And it reminded me of something else, another voice I was unable to silence...

Say my name

My mind was reeling, ready to erupt. I felt... I felt... bereft. Everything I had worked for, all that I had owned, was now gone. Gone. My life was an empty road, and there was no real destination in sight, just a false one, a pretend end to a faked quest towards a redemption that did not exist – that, indeed, had never existed.

"Let's go," I said, wondering how I was able to even speak under such conditions. The act continued; the movie went on; everything flowed towards the end game, whatever that might consist of.

We retraced our steps through the house, Manisa clinging to me as if I was keeping her upright. Her hands gripped me tightly, and I liked it. I did not want her to let go. We stepped outside and walked down the driveway, not once turning around to look back at the place. Manisa's parents were upstairs, long dead but not forgotten. She had said goodbye; there was no going back, not now, not ever.

Tallow was waiting for us as we turned and began to walk back towards the car. He was standing at the kerb and pointing what looked like some kind of sub-machine-gun in our direction; an automatic weapon that would tear us apart if we ran.

"Leave us alone. Just let us go. It's over." I stared at him; his bloody, thinning hair, his blasted expression. His face was slack, as if it were slipping from the bone beneath. The gun barrel lowered slowly, and he was unable to meet my gaze.

"Yes, it is." The voice did not belong to Tallow. It came from behind him, in the jeep he had backed up to the kerb. Tallow stepped sideways, to reveal Dr. Thwaite sitting in the rear of the jeep, a sawn-off shotgun clasped in each hand.

"Oh, shit. Shit. Shit." Manisa pressed against me, looking for safety. "I told them where we were going. I'm sorry…" She squeezed my arm, the fingers digging in deep.

Thwaite smiled. His face was horrible. The pain was etched like a tattoo across his features and his skin was white as paper. His lips were thin and pale; his teeth looked black. He smiled again. "I've come for her. The girl."

"You can't have her." I glared at him, beyond fear. I no longer even registered Tallow's presence. He was just the driver; he had delivered his package and faded out of sight.

Thwaite twitched. He was strapped with ropes and bandages into what looked like a bath chair, a small wicker mount that was secured inside the well at the back of the jeep by various lengths of bungee cord. He was wearing a gold lamé boob tube and a pair of tight moleskin shorts at least a size too small. The old favourite Mexican hat had been jammed onto his head at a rakish angle. His arms and legs were bare. He was all skin and bone. I realised that he could not move his body – the bullet in the small of his back must have caused a lot of damage to his spine. His skinny forearms were propped on his meatless thighs and the short-barrelled shotguns had been tied into his hands, so that he could hold them. His index fingers rested on the triggers.

"I've been meaning to ask you this since we met, you fucking nut-job." All my fear was gone; I had left it behind, in Manisa's parents' house. I was not being bold simply for the sake of it, but to prove a point. I just did not know what that point was. "What's with the stupid outfits?"

Thwaite grimaced; a spasm of pain tore a path across his face. "These outfits are a symbol of my ultimate freedom, an amusing way of announcing that I no longer belong to the old ways, the old world. They are my way of saying, 'this is me, and I am a new being'." He smiled through the pain, his eyes wet and wide and insane. I wondered what level of agony this camp maniac had gone through to be dressed by Tallow in those ugly shorts, that awful woman's top. I could barely even comprehend his motivation. The man was bat-shit crazy; this was a kind of madness I had not even guessed at until now.

"And this, dear boy, is the natty little outfit I've chosen to wear as I kill you."

CHAPTER 27

Thwaite's posture was twisted, as if his back had been thrown out of line. Yet somehow he managed to hold the shotguns steady. Despite having much of their barrels cut off, they must have been heavy. I almost admired the man's single-minded determination.

Behind and beyond Thwaite, along the street, a few figures had gathered. I had known they were there – the scattered bodies pointed to the fact that there had been a lot of leftover activity, and I suspected that at least some of them would have hung around looking for stragglers. They were intelligent enough for that kind of basic planning, and the continued self-mutilation must surely give them a little time to find someone to take with them when they pulled their own plugs.

Groups of them stood on a corner, at a main junction. There must have been two dozen of the bastards, maybe more. They stood and they watched us, realising that there was some kind of stand-off situation and biding their time to see how it panned out. No doubt they intended to fall upon the winners. They seemed restless, as if they wanted nothing more than to charge. The suicide urge must have been strong – I could see their feet shuffling and their hands grasping even at that distance.

"We have company," I said to the twisted vision of sartorial elegance before me. "Behind you."

Thwaite shook his head. "Come off it, man. This isn't a pantomime." One of the guns jittered in his grip. Manisa let out a tiny, subdued cry. I closed my eyes, expecting the blast.

"He isn't lying." It was Tallow, loyal and faithful Tallow, who was also by now completely mad. I wondered if I'd lost my mind, too, and I was just dragging Manisa along with me on an externalised tour of my inner turmoil.

"So what do we do now? If you shoot us, you're dead anyway. But if we stand together, we might have a chance of fighting them off." I stared at Thwaite, already knowing his answer.

"This is no longer about survival. It's about revenge. You destroyed my community. I have nothing left but Tallow, and he never was much good." Thwaite started to slide sideways in his chair, the bindings coming loose.

Tallow began to walk away. He dropped his gun and shuffled in the direction of the junction, where even more leftovers had gathered. There was a gang of them now, just waiting. Watching.

"Stupid bastard," said Thwaite, through gritted teeth. "I knew he'd leave me in the end." One of the shotguns dipped alarmingly. It was now pointed at the ground.

"You haven't got it in you. There's not enough strength in your body to pull the trigger. Don't be so stupid." It was true: Thwaite was no longer a threat. He was just a crazy old man in a clown's outfit, clinging on to something that he never really had in the first place.

We had won, but it was at best a pyrrhic victory. I wasn't yet sure what it had cost us, but knew that it would come to me eventually.

I took Manisa's hand and turned away, walking back towards the house. The leftovers were moving in now, coming towards us. They would reach Tallow first, and then Thwaite. That might give us enough time to barricade ourselves inside the house, and then try to think of another plan.

"Go straight through," said Manisa. "My dad's motorbike is parked in the back. He always keeps the tank full." She squeezed my hand. We were going to be okay… at least for now.

A shotgun went off behind us, and I heard the concrete footpath near my feet come apart in the explosion. Splinters of paving stone skipped past my legs, but I did not even twitch.

"Bastard!" Thwaite's voice was barely loud enough to be called a scream.

Manisa and I went inside and locked the door behind us. She led the way through the house, out the back door, grabbing a set of keys from a hook on the wall as we passed through the kitchen.

The motorbike was an old Honda, lovingly restored. Its paintwork shone in the sunlight, and I thanked Manisa's dead father for having such a useful hobby. He had saved our lives; I thought he might feel proud of that, if there was anything left of him to notice. I had never believed in the immortal soul, but right now I believed in irony as a form of saving grace.

Manisa climbed on the front and I sat behind her, clutching her waist. Again, I was aware that this was not exactly the traditional heroic way of doing things, but it seemed to me that she would be a better rider. I had only ever been on a motorbike once before, and that had been a silly little moped owned by an old university friend who delivered pizzas in the evening to make some extra cash.

Then, thinking of something useful, I got off and went back inside, where I searched through the drawers and cupboards in all the downstairs rooms until I found an AA road map tucked away in a bureau. I tore out the relevant pages before climbing back into position behind Manisa, and then we were finally ready to leave.

This was no time for the mindless posturing of false machismo. Pride was a luxury I could not even reach never mind afford.

The engine roared, and it was a good sound, a fine noise. It sounded like rejoicing.

We headed out of the open back gate, and just as we turned the corner into a narrow cobbled alley I heard another loud gunshot. Then I heard nothing but the motorbike's exhaust.

We covered the final leg of our journey in less than two hours. Such a small amount of time seemed absurd after all that we'd gone through. I navigated using my map pages, and we kept to the back roads, the dirt tracks and byways, keeping away from any populated areas. We met no further survivors along the way, and but for the distant sight of lumbering leftovers – small groups, or solitary figures silhouetted against the hills – we might have believed we were the last people left alive on earth. We saw dead bodies, of course, but by then we had grown accustomed to such sights. Death meant little to us; we were survivors.

The bike hugged the roads to the west of Sheffield, and we skirted the Peak District. We could hide there, I thought, if mine and Kay's home had been compromised. It might be a good place to get lost.

As we neared the end of our journey I wished that we could carry on forever, with an eternal destination never quite coming into view. If we searched until we died, it meant that we never had to discover the truth. We could pretend until the end of our days, playing this little game like kids sent away from the adults who had kept them close for far too many years to count.

But like all games, this one came to an end.

The road wound across the desolate moors, and I began to

recognise signs and landmarks. A lane, a hill, an old country graveyard, its scarred old stones leaning in just the way I remembered. Even the sky took on a shade that I knew well; the clouds shifted into familiar positions, forming shapes and formations into which I had stared so many times before, often describing them to Kay. To my wife.

My wife. I could barely even recall what she looked like.

The cottage appeared much the same as when I'd left it. The door was shut, the shutters over the windows locked firmly in place. I knew instantly that no leftovers had made it out this far, not yet – they had not strayed far from the cities and towns and villages. I wondered if other survivors sat huddled behind walls like these, weeping and wailing against the old masonry and praying for rescue.

"So this is it? This is home?" Manisa turned off the engine but stayed on the bike.

I swung my leg over the side and eased myself off the seat. "I guess so. It feels like... I dunno, like I've been gone for years."

Manisa smiled, but it was broken and twisted. "You have." I did not fully understand what she meant by that statement, but I grasped enough of her meaning not to argue the point.

Birds sang in the trees. The sky was low and rather lovely. It looked as if everything was perfect here, that death had not yet extended its reach to this secluded place. But I knew different; I knew the lie of what I saw before me. "I'd better go in." I touched Manisa's arm, expecting her to pull away. But she did not move.

"Go on," she said, softly. "I'll be here when you get back. I'm not going anywhere. I have nowhere left to go."

I turned away so she could not see my tears. It felt wrong somehow to weep, as if to do so would be just another white lie in a long line of untruths. My feet crunched on the gravel as I trod the path to the front door, feeling as if I'd never been away yet had not been home for ages. The emotion was intense and confusing, and I felt giddy for a moment. I stopped at the door and leaned against the frame, touching the flaking timber and letting it ground me in a reality that had never really gone away.

Say my name

I fumbled for my key and unlocked the door, then pushed it slowly open. Slowly because I did not want to rush this, any part of it. I wanted the moment to last forever...I wanted to be poised at the threshold for a thousand lifetimes. Maybe that would change things, or even turn back the clocks.

I said her name, as requested: "Kay." The sound came back at me from the darkness, a distortion of my own voice.

The hallway was a throat that was swallowing me. I felt myself being pulled along and sucked inside. The door remained open behind me but in my mind it closed forever, shutting out the rest of the world. Part of me had never left this place – a shade, a shadow, a slice of me I had barely even missed. I saw it moving across the rough walls, the bare boards of the floor, and towards the cellar door. My own ghost loomed there, waiting for the rest of me to catch up. Haunting all of my yesterdays, todays and tomorrows.

"Kay."

I was standing at the cellar door before I even realised that I'd moved towards it. I reached out, felt the grain of the wood, and pressed my palm against it. Once again I took out my keys and located the correct one. The big one: the old one. The key to everything.

I unlock the door.

I push it open.

Then I enter.

The concrete steps are so very steep, and I have to hold on to the wall as I make my way down into the cellar. The banister broke away from the wall over a year ago, when I manoeuvred the old fridge-freezer down here with the help of a belligerent delivery man.

The steps are cold; I feel the chill as it travels up my legs and into my crotch.

The light flickers rapidly when I pull the cord. I recall this faulty connection from before I left – indeed, I am starting to let myself remember so much more as well. Finally, I am allowing myself to remember.

To remember it all.

I reach the bottom of the cellar steps and stand at the point where the wall turns at a right angle. The air is cool and stale, but I can taste her. I can taste my wife. The room is damp, but I can smell her perfume. I sprayed a lot of it down here before I left. I had to disguise the stench.

Reaching out with one hand and grasping the edge of the wall, I pull myself around to face the thing I have run from and now have run back to in the hope that it might be different, that it might have changed. That everything might have changed for the better.

Kay is right where I left her, hanging from the ceiling beam. Hanging by her lovely neck.

Her body has long since stopped spinning in that badly-lit, almost airless space, and her feet are pointed toes-down towards the floor. One shoe off, one shoe on. The suicide note – the one she spray-painted on the wall, taunts me all over again:

Say my name.

But I can't. Not now.

Shuffling forward to stand at her side, I stare at what I have refused to admit for so long, even to myself. Kay hanged herself a week ago, before any of this even began. The miscarriage – her third – was too much of a burden to carry, and she chose this way out to spare herself yet another failed pregnancy. She knew that I would want to try again, and she would, too, but it was more than she could stand.

All those faked calls I made on my mobile, the text messages I sent myself, the lies I played out inside my head... all of it done simply to push this sight from my mind, to pretend that it has not happened.

That it never happened.

That it will not happen.

We never told any of our friends about the miscarriage, and I kept the news of her death to myself, allowing it to eat me up inside and turn me into someone I no longer recognise. A madman already on the road to oblivion, even before the rest of the world caught up.

It was all about control.

In the end, that's what broke me: the all-consuming need to take charge of a life that was by now too far beyond control. There was never anything that I could do to prevent this. It was a tragedy waiting to happen, and the timing was *immaculate*.

My wife killed herself. But she did it before the rest of them.

Her eyes are not black; they are blue, just as they always were. Blue and dim and distant, like a cloudless sky in a film seen long ago, when we were both kids.

The suicide plague – or whatever the hell it is – has not touched her; *life* has touched her, and bent her out of shape, and finally snapped her.

Life killed her as it will kill us all.

My wife.

My beauty.

My world.

It all came to an end even before the end began.

I recall scraping what was left of He-She out of the bath, weeping into my fist as I rinsed away the bloody water and then watching in painful silence as it drained down the plug hole. I remember listening to the awful sound of Kay screaming in another room, and closing my eyes to pray to the empty darkness I found there as she began to smash plates and cups and ornaments against the walls.

Finally she retreated inside herself, curling up somewhere I could not reach her. Then, one morning, as I drove to the nearest town to pick up some fresh bread and a pint of the goats' milk we both liked, because she'd asked for them, saying that she finally felt well enough to eat, she made the lonely walk down into the cellar, threw a length of rope over a high beam, and leapt off a small pine box that she had carried down with her.

The box contains our wedding photos. It is still there, off to one side, overturned and with the photos spread out like dead memories across the cellar floor.

I found her an hour later, cold and dead and still swinging. The message was daubed on the wall next to her; an old joke we had shared, a comforting mantra meant for whenever one of us got scared without the other.

"Just say my name. Say my name and I'll be there. Say my name."

I say her name again, but this time I am still scared. This time I am terrified.

Say my name

And then I can't. Not ever again.

I just can't say it.

This is how the world ends.

CODA

It has been three months now since Manisa died; three long months I have spent on my own, fighting against the cold and the loneliness and the miles of empty countryside. The babies were barely even formed when they tore their way out of her womb, killing her as they killed themselves.

But they were just about formed enough that I saw their small black eyes in their dough-white faces.

Manisa died smiling. She did not know that the twins were leftovers: she thought that she had given them life as she slipped away. It hurts when I think of this. It hurts a lot. So I try to pretend it never happened, just as I pretended that Kay did not kill herself... until the truth could no longer be held at bay.

The truth. All of it.

I buried Manisa and the twins on the moor, next to Kay's shallow grave, and not far from the place where I made a small grave for the scrappy remains of He-She.

I have spent too long burying my dead, it seems, and now there is nobody left here to bury me. I know that I should move on, but where would I go? I have not seen a leftover since we arrived here, nor have I seen any sign of further survivors.

I am alone. There is nobody here but me, and the thoughts of what might have been.

At night I stare at the sky and pretend that I am the only one left alive on Earth. Occasionally I see a shooting star, and I turn to the ghosts of my loved ones – both of them, Kay and Manisa – and I wish that they could see it, too.

I am running low on wine. I try not to drink during the day, but the nights seem to grow longer now that I am totally alone. Wine fills the gaps; it stops me from remembering too much.

Last night it began to snow: fat white flakes drifting like old promises down from the black night sky. I put out my tongue and I caught one, balancing it there. I held it for as long as I could, desperate for it to keep its shape and not melt away, like everything melts away. But soon enough the flake turned to water, dripping down my chin and into my beard. Nothing ever lasts, it all changes state. Ice becomes water. Love becomes loss. Hate changes into something that feels like love…

After the snowflake, I went and sat again by the graves, drinking wine directly from the bottle and singing an old blues song – one Kay had loved and that I hoped Manisa might have enjoyed, if she had lived to hear it. I stayed there for hours after the song ended, waiting for the sun to come up. Then I came back inside and wrote some more in my diary. It's all I have left now, and the thought that one day someone might read it fills me with a weird kind of relief.

I suppose we all want to leave something behind, even if it is just a spray-painted message on a cellar wall or the ghost of a smile on cold, dead lips.

My mind turns often to the situation beyond my tiny domain; to the leftovers and the few scattered survivors who must surely be out there. It is my guess that humanity has experienced a sort of reverse Big Bang, where extinction and not creation was the ultimate goal. There was no outside agency involved; this is a truly manmade apocalypse.

I still do not have a gun – my irregular foraging expeditions into the surrounding area have unearthed no firearms. I do, however, have a machete. It would be hard to kill myself with a machete, but one day I might just be desperate enough to try. Until then, I shall carry on watching the skies for shooting stars and speaking with the ghosts of the dead. I shall sit and drink wine and laugh into the darkness, knowing that even though the end came I endured, I carried on. I keep going.

I carry on, and for the life of me I do not know why. I have no idea why.

No idea at all.

Author's Afterword

The initial idea for this short novel came to me when I stumbled across some rather disturbing footage on the BBC News website. Using a camera in a mobile phone, someone had filmed a strange event.

Two European women were spotted walking along the hard shoulder of a busy motorway – it may have been the M25, but I can't remember exactly. These women suddenly walked out into the traffic, calmly trying to throw themselves under the wheels of passing vehicles. Cars and vans and trucks swerved to avoid them, some of them stopped and the drivers got out to help guide the women off the road to safety. But these two women didn't want to be moved: they actually fought against their would-be saviours, striking and kicking out whilst still attempting to dive in front of the traffic. Their faces, even at a distance, were impassive. The women were not ranting or raving. They knew exactly what they were doing.

One woman was successfully pinned down by a group of men at the side of the motorway.

Her companion made a break for it, ran across the busy carriageway, leapt over the central reservation, and was hit by a van or a lorry or a bus (again, the exact details elude me) travelling in the opposite direction.

The footage was horrifying. I had never seen anything quite like it. It was the calmness that hit me hardest, the way the women were completely unflappable as they tried to kill themselves. What – if anything – was going through their minds? What was motivating them to do this?

The incident nagged at me for a long time, invading my sleep and running in a constant loop through my dreams. So, as most writers do, I started to write it out of my system. *The End* is the result of this lengthy process, and the opening sequence is actually a rough approximation of what I saw in that shaky handheld footage.

Other influences began to take hold as I worked my way into the novel. George Romero's *The Crazies* is an obvious stepping off point, along with David Cronenberg's *Rabid*; but all of those gritty little plague movies from the late 1970s (and their slim novelizations) had something to do with the ultimate direction of the piece. Those films – short, brutal, grungy and blessed with a social conscience – fuelled my writing and helped guide me. I hope the finished book does them justice; they certainly darkened my youth with their grim message.

Inspiration also came from the early apocalyptic novels of J.G. Ballard. Yet more slender volumes, but they contained within them a world of terror. In a uniquely English way, Ballard essayed mankind's downfall, many times, and it had never seemed so forlorn, so bitter-sweet. Far from being afraid of such end-of-days events, I secretly longed for them.

The End is, I suppose, a synthesis of all these influences, but it's also its own beast: a gritty little end-of-the-world credit-crunch-inspired scenario that hopefully goes for your throat, and then climbs down it...

In an ideal world this novel would be published in pocket paperback format and cost you less than a fiver in your local bookshop. But this isn't an ideal world, and sadly that beloved format seems to have been abandoned by the publishing industry. It's our loss. My loss. My childhood memories are filled with small books that always fitted so neatly into the back pocket of my faded blue jeans. And all those memories look like scenes from *The Crazies* – jagged, grainy, dark-tinted, and filled with a wonderful sense of threat.

I hope *The End* scared you.

I hope it *scarred* you.

This was how their world ended.

The Bitten Word
Edited by Ian Whates

All new tales of vampiric horror, with front cover art by John Kaiine and back cover art by award-winning artist Les Edwards.

Available as an A5 paperback £9.99
And a Special Signed Hardback edition, limited to just 150 numbered copies, signed by all the authors £32.00

The limited edition hardback includes a bonus story by Ian Watson, plus a colour plate of Les Edwards' back cover picture, *Descending*.

Stories by:
Kelley Armstrong, Tanith Lee, Freda Warrington, Simon Clark, Gary McMahon, Jon Courtenay Grimwood, Gail Z Martin, Sarah Singleton, Storm Constantine, Nancy Kilpatrick, Chaz Brenchley, Kari Sperring, Sam Stone, Andrew Hook, Donna Scott, John Kaiine, Ian Whates and (in the hardback only) **Ian Watson**.

noir

edited by Ian Whates

Thirteen stories that dance around genre boundaries but are linked by a sense of foreboding, a prickly itch that will unsettle and leave you with the impression of something sinister lurking just beyond the reach of awareness...

Dark science fiction, the supernatural, puzzling mysteries and shocking twists from:

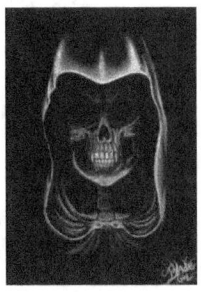

E.J. Swift
Adam Roberts
Donna Scott
Emma Coleman
Paula Wakefield
Simon Kurt Unsworth
Jay Caselberg
Marie O'Regan
Paul Graham Raven
Simon Morden
James Worrad
Paul Kane
Alex Dally MacFarlane

Welcome to the dark side....!

la femme

The companion volume to *Noir*
Edited by Ian Whates

For anyone who still considers woman to be the weaker sex…
Think again.

Twelve stories of dark science fiction, the supernatural, blood-rich fantasy, puzzling mysteries and shocking twists from:

Stephen Palmer, Frances Hardinge, Storm Constantine, Andrew Hook, Adele Kirby, Stewart Hotston, John Llewellyn Probert, Jonathan Oliver, Maura McHugh, Holly Ice, Ruth Booth, Benjanun Sriduangkaew

"*La Femme* is a very strong collection and highly recommended."
— *Amazing Stories.*

www.newconpress.co.uk

NEWCON PRESS

Publishing quality Science Fiction, Fantasy, Dark Fantasy and Horror for eight years and counting.

Winner of the 2010 'Best Publisher' Award from the European Science Fiction Society.

Anthologies, novels, short story collections, novellas, paperbacks, hardbacks, signed limited editions, e-books…
Why not take a look at some of our other titles?

Neil Gaiman, Brian Aldiss, Kelley Armstrong, Alastair Reynolds, Stephen Baxter, Christopher Priest, Tanith Lee, Joe Abercrombie, Dan Abnett, Nina Allan, Sarah Ash, Neal Asher, Tony Ballantyne, James Barclay, Chris Beckett, Lauren Beukes, Aliette de Bodard, Chaz Brenchley, Keith Brooke, Eric Brown, Pat Cadigan, Jay Caselberg, Michael Cobley, Storm Constantine, Hal Duncan, Jaine Fenn, Paul di Filippo, Jonathan Green, Jon Courtenay Grimwood, Frances Hardinge, Gwyneth Jones, M. John Harrison, Amanda Hemingway, Paul Kane, Leigh Kennedy, Kim Lakin-Smith, David Langford, Alison Littlewood, James Lovegrove, Una McCormack, Sophia McDougall, Gary McMahon, Alex Dally MacFarlane, Ken MacLeod, Ian R MacLeod, Gail Z Martin, Juliet E McKenna, John Meaney, Simon Morden, Mark Morris, Anne Nicholls, Stan Nicholls, Marie O'Regan, Philip Palmer, Stephen Palmer, Sarah Pinborough, Robert Reed, Rod Rees, Andy Remic, Mike Resnick, Mercurio D Rivera, Adam Roberts, Justina Robson, Stephanie Saulter, Gaie Sebold, Robert Shearman, Sarah Singleton, Martin Sketchley, Kari Sperring, Benjanun Sriduangkaew, Brian Stapleford, Charles Stross, Tricia Sullivan, EJ Swift, Adrian Tchaikovsky, Steve Rasnic Tem, Lavie Tidhar, Lisa Tuttle, Simon Kurt Unsworth, Ian Watson, Freda Warrington, Liz Williams, Neil Williamson, and many more.

Join our mailing list to get advance notice of new titles, book launches and events, and receive special offers on books.

www.newconpress.co.uk

Immanion Press

Independent publisher of horror, fantasy and science fiction since 2003

Para Kindred, edited by Storm Constantine and Wendy Darling.

The androgynous and mysterious Wraeththu have risen to replace humanity upon a ravaged world. Based on the world created by Storm Constantine for her Wraeththu novels, the stories in this collection explore bizarre mutations and specialisations that have arisen, hidden within the developing Wraeththu tribes and throughout the corners of the world. Shape-shifters, semi-mythological beings, or hara who have evolved in other unexpected ways, *Para Kindred* features stories from ten writers, and includes two new stories each by Storm Constantine and Wendy Darling. *Featuring stories by: Storm Constantine, Wendy Darling, Martina Bellovičová, Ash Corvida, Nerine Dorman, Suzanne Gabriel, Fiona Lane, Maria J Leel, Daniela Ritter and E S Wynn.* 978-1-907737-60-2 £11.99 paperback

Turquoiselle by Tanith Lee

Not much is what it seems. The job can be dull, but quite demanding – it involves a lot of driving, often very long hours, an always erratic schedule. Not to mention social duties with certain important clients. The work is lucrative, however. He can easily afford the house in Kent, and the costly wants of Donna, his partner. For someone like Carver, dragged up through a deprived and abused childhood, not such a bad achievement. It's just that suddenly things are running less smoothly. This stuff with Donna… Various unusual tensions at work… the bizarre and threatening business over Silvia… In the end, maybe all you can rely on is yourself. A dark speculative thriller, this is the seventh in Tanith Lee's captivating The Colouring Book series. 978-1-907737-59-6 £11.99 paperback

http://www.immanion-press.com
info@immanion-press.com